Firstly I want to thank Jehovah for blessing me with the ability to tell stories. Without him, none of the things I've accomplished would've been possible. I would love to give thanks to my Mother, Tara Lipscomb for always supporting me in anything I do. My Aunt Timea for always pushing me to reach any goals I set for myself. My sister Desiree, although we fight every day, for making sure I excel in everything. She's a motivation. My Ace, Ashley Harris, for making sure I kept my head in the books during my last year of High School. My grandma Mommy for making sure I let everyone know about my books. My promoter! My bestfriend Damonte, you was up listening to these stories come to fruition. If wasn't for the *bachelor pad*, this story wouldn't have even ̶ ̶ ̶ ̶ ̶ ̶ ̶ LMAO. (insider)

And thank you to all my readers w. money on my books. I appreciate all the love and support. With any of your support, none of this would have happened. Thank you to Mr. Riggs and Ms. Jenkins for being the greatest teachers I've ever bonded with. Ms. Jenkins you are a hero of mine for simply being a shoulder I could lean on & talk too at one of the lowest points of my life. Because of you, I've learned so much about myself and the strength and passion I have to conquer my dreams. I'm forever indebted to the support you've shown me.

Also by Bronchey (Ju'Tone Sair) Battle

Billionaire Boyz

Gangsta' Bitch

Seduced by The Hustle

Seducing The Hustle

Epilogue

We sat inside Herahm's white 2016 Ferrari Laferrari in front of the park with Ty Dolla Sign's Paranoid playing softly in the background. The song was definitely befitting for the occasion, since the last time I was in the presence of him, we were not on the best of terms. My instincts were at an all-time high and something about this situation didn't feel right to me. My instincts had never steered me wrong before, and I just couldn't shake the nerves.

"Germany!" He said, pulling me out of my thoughts.

"Wassup Herahm? What is it exactly that you need to say to me?" I asked.

"I have you out here to see if we could possibly fix what was broken in our relationship."

"Herahm, you have to be fucking kidding me! You cheated on me and got a bitch pregnant! You really think I want yo dirty dick ass after some *shit like that? Get the fuck outta here." I rolled my eyes at his black ass and turned my head.*

"Look Germany, I don't know how many times I have to apologize to make this right, but I can't or won't live without you."

There was a underlying message in what he just said, and I felt it.

"You don't have a choice, because I'm all the way done. You don't even realize how much I loved you. Would have done anything for you! I worshipped the ground you walked on. When you were happy, I was happy. When you were hurting, so was I. Your smile made me melt. The way you held me made me weak. The way you touched me drove me crazy. But the moment you started sharing yourself with every other bitch, you became less special."

Tears began falling at this point, but I finally had the chance to tell him how much he hurt me and I couldn't stop.

"I don't want you anymore Herahm," I finished, wiping the tears from my eyes. "I asked you that day we were in the bed when I woke up in

the middle of the night to not hurt me. And this is the shit you do!"

"Germany, I'm sorry, please believe me. Do you remember the first time we met? It was two years ago in the same park we're in right now. Why you think I brought you here? I want to fix this."

"NO! What the fuck did I just tell you. There is nothing to fucking fix! It's over, so shut the fuck up talking to me! I gotta get the fuck outta here," I yelled. All the hatred I had for him began bubbling to the surface, and I needed this nigga out of my presence.

"Germany-Skyy Santana!" He started, adding fuel to the fire.

"If you don't shut the fuck up, I'm getting the fuck out."

"You better stop cutting me off while I'm fucking talking!" He warned, before continuing, "like I was about to say, I won't live without you Germany. You belong to me!" A crazy look glazed over his eyes and it was unsettling.

"Fuck it, I'm gone." I spat in his face and flung my door open.

"Germany!" he yelled, hopping out of the car behind me.

I continued walking and never turned around to see whether he was following behind me or not. The sounds of my Jimmy Choos click clacking on the pavement beneath me sounded off in the deserted lot. By time I finally turned around, it was too late.

BAM! He hit me on the side of my head with the butt of his gun. I went crashing straight to the ground.

Oh my god, he's going to kill me, was the first thought that crossed my mind.

"Bitch I tried to keep it simple with yo mu'fucking ass, but you just don't know how to act. I told you I wouldn't live without you and I meant that shit." He stood above me with his silver plated pistol pointing directly at my mouth.

"I'mma pop you right in yo fucking grill since yo mouth so fucking greasy."

Before I could even beg for my life the next thing I heard was the blast of a gun.

Chapter One

Two Years Earlier

"I just a need a hundred to be able to pay my rent," I begged my mom as we sat at the local *Applebees*.

"What's going on with your hours at that stupid store you're working at?" She quizzed.

"*Forever 21* aint giving up no hours ma."

"My poor Germany, if you only knew how to use your assets to your advantage. You wouldn't be stuck in this position," she huffed, pulling the money out of her purse.

"Not this again ma, I know what I look like, but that doesn't mean I need to use my looks to get ahead. I will make my own way in this world without asking a man for anything. **THAT**, will only get you so far... *You should know*," I said, whispering the last part under my breath.

"Okay smart ass, you say all of that but you sitting here asking me for money."

I rolled my eyes as I looked from the burnt orange colored *Hermes* bag she was rocking, to the diamond studs she had in her ears. Armenian and Black, my mother was absolutely stunning. Light brown complexion with emerald green eyes and a head full of sleek jet black hair, Moms never had trouble with the fellas.

"I saw you roll your eyes at me young lady. All I'm saying is; you are beautiful Germany. Even more beautiful than me, and you know mama a bad bitch!" We both started laughing before she continued, "but seriously babe, you are. Once you start to believe it, the world is yours. You have that beautiful light brown complexion with those beautiful eyes we both inherited from your grandmother. All that hair, and to add, you are mixed with Vietnamese. Your eyes are colored and slanted. Girl bye! Once you get rid of them glasses and those loose ass clothes you wear, it's on."

"I hear you ma, I really do." I said, hoping she'd just shut up. We had this same conversation so often, I knew it by heart. Truth is, I knew I was beautiful. I didn't look like any of the other girls from around the way and I was told that often. But growing up with a mother who had a different male companion every other week, beauty was something I tended to run from. I didn't want to be that female that changed my man like I changed my underwear. When I was ready to unleash the beast that lay dormant underneath the glasses and sweaters I wore, it'd be for the right reasons.

Our lunch continued as usual until we went our separate ways.

Back at home in my one bedroom apartment, I ran through my homework, while periodically checking the time. It was the night of the annual charity basketball game in Oakland and I knew I needed to be there. Being a full-time student at the *Arts Institute of San Francisco*, while also working a dead-end job, I never had time to get out. I was getting ready to graduate, and another step towards getting my shit together. But tonight, I had to make an exception.

7:00pm rolled around a lot faster than I anticipated. I had just finished my sketches for my fashion design class when my phone rang.

"Hey girl," I answered, putting my earphones in my ear as I walked into my bedroom.

"You getting ready?" My sister Brooklyn asked from the other end of the phone.

"I just finished getting my homework done, so now I'm in this closet tryna find something to throw on."

"Well I'm half way done getting ready so most likely I'll probably end up meeting you up there."

"That's fine, it wont take me long."

"You talked to daddy?"

That caught me completely off guard. "No, where that come from?"

"He called me today tryna play daddy," she laughed. "Trying to question me about what I been up too, and what I should be doing. On some blah blah shit."

"Nah, bruh know not to hit my phone with that bullshit. I done had enough of one parent for the day so I refuse to hear shit from his absent ass. Nigga should have been hollering about some coins, the fuck!" We burst out cracking up.

"Right, but get dress because I should be leaving in about twenty minutes."

"Okay."

We hung up and I raced to the shower. Lathering my towel with body wash, I thoroughly cleaned myself while thinking about what I'd throw on once I got out. Mentally traveling through my closet, I knew I wanted to be comfortable but my Moms words also kept playing in my head.

Getting out the shower, I stood in my closet in just my towel. I kept avoiding the floor-length mirror that was built into the closet to stop myself from staring at my reflection. I tried to avoid it until I couldn't anymore. I dropped the towel from my body and stood there naked.

Standing at 5'6", light brown complexion with sleek jet black hair that hung to the middle of my back, you'd have to be blind to mistake my beauty. C-cup breast, flat as a board stomach with a set of thick thighs and an ass that Stevie Wonder couldn't miss, I was a dime.

"You gone be something so vicious when you get older." The voice kept repeating in my head.

I removed my glasses from my eyes and stared into them deeply. A single tear slid down and my face and I turned from my reflection.

I threw on a pair of black sweats, a hoodie and some Timbs. My hair was in a high bun. I put on my white-gold bottom grill and headed out the door.

Inside of my burgundy 2008 Toyota Avalon, I turned the key over to hear no engine start. "You gotta be fucking kidding me!" I turned the key over once more to get the same result. "What the fuck!"

Grabbing my iPhone out of my purse, I hurriedly dialed Brooklyn. Please pick up, I whispered just as she answered the phone. "Please tell me you haven't left yet!"

"I'm walking out the door now. What's wrong?"

"Bitch my fucking car won't start! Come get me."

"You lucky we live a block from each other," she laughed before we hung up.

Five minutes later I was seated cozily in her 2004 Honda Accord headed to East Oakland.

"What the fuck are you wearing Germany?"

"Some sweats?"

"Exactly. You out here dressed like a bum knowing it's gone be hella niggas out here."

"Girl bye." I rolled my eyes.

She had *Shake that Monkey* by Too Short blasting out of the two 10's in her trunk. Her long hombre colored hair was parted down the middle and was swinging from side to side as she bounced in her seat. Brooklyn was ten months younger than me and I loved my sister to death. Her yellow complexion, asian eyes, and slim thick frame, my sis was bomb. We met when I was 10, after not even knowing each other existed, but once we did, we were inseparable.

"Turn that up, you know that's my song." She turned it up and we turned up all the way to the game.

We turned heads as soon as we stepped into the building. Brooklyn, standing at 5'4", had on a pair of denim overalls that she left hanging in the front. A white long-sleeve half shirt and a pair of wheat colored timbs. We luckily came across two open seats in the front row and immediately snagged em.

The Jaguars, which was the home team was trailing behind by three points. Guy after guy stepped to us as we attempted to watch the game. A light skin dude had caught Brooklyn's eye, because next thing I knew, I was sitting by myself as she moved to the other end of the court to chop it up with him.

I sat watching the game for awhile until a dark-skinned cutie with gray eyes copped a squat next to me.

"Wassup gorgeous," he greeted, turning his body to face me.

"Hello," I greeted, while discreetly looking him up and down. His right arm was covered in tattoos, and he had silver bottoms in his mouth. His hair was cut in a clean fade, and he had some of the prettiest hair I'd ever seen on a dark-skin nigga. He wore all black with a pair of pony leopard Louboutins on his feet.

"May I get your name?" His gray eyes were hypnotizing.

"Germany, and yourself?"

"I'm Herahm, my pleasure to make your acquaintance. And I'm sure you get this often, but your eyes are beautiful."

I started blushing before replying, "thank you. It's funny because I was just thinking the same thing about yours."

"Thanks beautiful. I'm not trying to get too personal… yet, but why you sitting out here alone? I know ya man's must've wandered off somewhere for a minute because I know you not out here by yourself."

"Yet?" I laughed. "That was cute how you just tried to slide that up in there. But I'm here with my sister," I replied, pointing in Brooklyn's direction.

"Oh okay, she over there chopping it with my young nigga Maurice."

"I guess," I replied, turning back to the game. I noticed some of the females had begun giving me salty looks, and I could only imagine it had something to do with the slick talking nigga seated next to me.

"Did I do something wrong?" He asked.

"Not at all, just noticed some of your fans been giving me the evil eye so I'm just watching my surroundings."

"A woman who doesn't let her guard down in the presence of the unknown? I like that."

"I'm sure." He kept tryna make small talk but something about these females was just throwing me off. I caught them ice grilling me then turning their attention to Brooklyn. But once them three big burly bitches started making their way towards Brooklyn, I already knew what time it was.

"Excuse me," I said, getting from my seat as I followed behind those three bitches who were walking up on my sister.

"Wassup bitch!" I heard the leader of the three yell to Brooklyn. Brooklyn without a second thought punched that bitch in her face and it was on. I snatched up both of the bitches who were with the other one and tagged that ass.

Growing up in Sunnydale, bitches use to pick with me often because I was pretty. But this pretty bitch can run with the best of em. I two pieced the big bitch with the singles in her head and then squared up with the other one.

"Bitch yo weak ass gone sneak up from behind!" Yelled the one wearing the baby phat outfit.

"So wassup?" I said, right before I clocked her in her nose. Blood gushed out like a leaking faucet. I followed that with two jabs before that bitch dropped.

I ran over to where Brooklyn and the other bitch was chunking em and kicked that bitch in her back. "You got my sister fucked up bitch!" I yelled, grabbing that hoe by her weave. I rammed my fist into that bitch face repeatedly until the bitch with the braids came and pulled me by my bun. She snuck me with a good one to the cheek, I recovered and rushed that bitch to the ground. I was on top of her raining haymakers to her face.

Bitches like this always seemed to take me out of my element. I kept punching her until I felt somebody pulling me off of her. I was ready to swing again when I realized it was Herahm.

"Relax lil mama, you got em."

"Fuck all of that, where the fuck is my sister?" By this time it was complete chaos going on, and I knew all too well how this shit was about to end. We was deep in the East, and them niggas shoot guns like it was a sport.

"She right here," he said, pointing to Brooklyn who was headed to the car with Maurice in tow.

"I gotta go!"

I ran to the car behind Brooklyn just as the bullets started flying. "Drive bitch!" I yelled as we peeled out of there.

"Who the fuck was those bitches?" She asked, as we hopped on the freeway headed back to San Francisco.

"I have no idea, but they got what they was looking for."

"Girl yo ass was fighting two at once!" She laughed.

"I mean, shit we had to divide em and you was already fighting that big bitch so I took off!"

"Thanks for having my back sis."

"I always will!"

Chapter Two

"… Today is the beginning of your future, young people. Everything you do from this moment on will shape your tomorrow. Remember that. Congratulations to the *Arts Institute of San Francisco* class of '13. Let's get a huge round of applause for all of the graduates!" Concluded Mr. Sorintini, the President of our school.

I really did it. I graduated college, I kept thinking to myself. I was overcome with so much happiness. To accomplish my dream of graduating college, I was ecstatic.

Wiping the tears that had accumulated away, I came back to reality just in time to toss our caps in the air to conclude the ceremony.

"Germany I am so proud of you." My Mom said snapping photos of me.

"Thanks Ma."

"You want to go out to celebrate?" She asked.

"No. I'm gonna go home, throw on some sweats and call it a night. I have to work tomorrow," I replied, cleaning my glasses with my gown.

"I love you baby."

"I love you too Mom."

Chapter Three

It's been a week since graduation, and two weeks since the brawl at the game and things had begun to go back to normal. Working this eight hour shift at *Forever 21*, I was so fed up with this job. I made just enough to get by, and it wasn't cutting it.

I finished ringing up my last customer before I took my break when I heard my supervisor requesting me through the mic in my ear.

"What's going on Shannon?" I asked, walking into her office.

"I need you to work through your break Germany. Susan got sick and needed to leave so there isn't anyone who can cover the floor."

"I've been here since nine this morning. It's going on *2:00pm*. How am I not gonna get a lunch?"

"I mean, if it's a big deal, you can leave and not return."

I was two seconds from just walking out until thoughts of rent and my shitty ass car came into play.

"I guess," I said before I stood and stormed out.

"Yes bitch, I made two racks last night just from dancing in two hours." I heard a customer say.

"Damn girl, it be jumping like that in *Exquisite*?"

"Sure does," the girl retorted. She turned to me and said, "excuse me, do you work here?"

I took a deep breath, put a smile on my face and walked over to the pair.

"Yes I do, how may I help you two ladies today?"

"Do you guys have this in a small?" She asked, holding up a black and white striped dress with sheer fabric on the sides.

"We just might, follow me this way," I answered her, leading them in the direction of the dress.

"Girl do you see her ass? This bitch would make a killing at the club. Niggas in there love them exotic looking bitches."

I acted as if I hadn't heard the girl whispering about me as I showed them the dresses.

"There should be a small in here somewhere."

"Do you like your job?" She asked me.

I discreetly looked her up and down. She had a pair of baby blue ripped jeans, a white v-neck shirt with a fur vest on top. Nude Louboutins on her feet. Brown skin female with twists in her head.

"I mean, its fine I guess." I answered.

"Well I'm no hating ass bitch so I'll get straight to the point. You are beautiful. I work at *Exquisite* gentlemen's club and I know a bitch like you would make a killing in there. Whenever you get tired of working for this chump change, go check it out. You are twenty-one right?"

"Twenty-three, but I'm straight. Thanks though, and if I can help you with anything else, let me know."

I walked away not knowing if I should be offended or slightly flattered. *The fact that she offered me to become a stripper though? The fuck.*

"Germany you can finally take your break, Hannah is here now!" Shannon said to me, coming out of the office. The bitch rolled her eyes and went back to her office.

"Better be," I said walking straight out the door.

The rest of the work day went by smooth, and being back in my apartment, I couldn't wait to just relax.

Just as I was to hop in the shower, my phone got to ringing. "Yes," I answered, after peeping my caller ID.

"Bitch! We going the fuck out tonight! So I'm on my way to your house to take you shopping for some new shit. Maurice gave me some money so I'm about to spend some of it on you a new wardrobe. *Exquisite* suppose to be packed tonight and I already got us free access inside. Drake, Meek Mill, and Lil Wayne suppose to be there." Brooklyn yelled excitedly. "So be outside in two minutes."

"Girl I had a long day, aint nobody trying to be in the club all night. A strip club at that. Bitch I aint gay!"

"Girl you going and I'll be by there to pick you up." *Click.*

I just can't catch a break! Throwing my phone on the bed, I turned on my heels to head out the door when my phone rang again.

"What?!" I yelled, not even bothering to look at my caller ID.

"Miss Nguyen, this is Jeff with *Fast Paced Auto* calling, because you are late on your payments and we are outside to repossess your car."

Oh my gosh, I totally forgot about that. I raced outside to the sight of yelling flashing lights in front of my apartment. The tow truck had my car hooked up already and I just wanted to break down.

"Please sir, I just graduated college. Please don't do this." I begged.

"Sorry, there's nothing I can do." The white driver responded, pushing the button to move my car to the top of his truck.

Brooklyn pulled up just as the driver took off. Shaking my head, I hopped in the car and cried.

I need some money, and fast! I thought.

By *10:00pm*, Brooklyn and I were strutting through *Exquisite*. It was a full house since everybody knew the ballers would be in the building. Dressed in a white body suit, jean shorts, and white Jeffrey Campbell boots, I was definitely dressed for the occasion. A white blazer draped my shoulders with loose curls in my head.

Bust a Nut by Biggie played in the background as the women in the establishment danced to pay their bills. I watched in amazement as one of the dancers climbed to the top of the pole as another dancer climbed underneath her and planked on the pole. The first dancer slid back down on the pole and landed on top of the second. The bitch started clapping her ass to the beat of the song as the other dancer began spiraling around the pole.

Money of all denominations began flying onto the stage. They were bad!

"Y'all make some noise. We got Wayne, Luda, and Tip in the building!" The DJ screamed over the music.

It was like the scene on *The Players Club* when Uncle Luke walked in. All the dancers came from the back onto the floor to get that money.

"Look at that ass stampeding," I laughed, mocking Alex Thomas from the movie.

Brooklyn, catching on, starting cracking.

"You slow!"

"I'm about to get a drink. You want anything?"

"A shot of Ciroc and lemonade."

"I got you."

I made my way to the bar, being hounded down by the thirsty patrons in the establishment every step of the way.

"Can I get two shots of Ciroc and lemonade!" I ordered, once I made it to the bar.

"Ten dollars." The bartender responded.

"Put it on my tab Alex." I turned to see the female I met earlier in the day at work.

"So you came to check it out after-all," she greeted, as I grabbed the drinks off the bar.

"Yeah, I came to see what the hype is about. But being here, girl I see what's happening."

"I'm sorry, my name is Keyshia. I'm sitting here holding a whole ass conversation with you and you don't even know my name."

"I'm Germany, pleasure to meet," I giggled.

Keyshia had bills of all denominations hanging from her garter. She must've caught me eyeballing her cash because she hollered, "right,

I'm making a killing tonight. I'm telling you , if you came through, you'd be straight."

"The way I'm feeling, shit I just might try it out!"

"If you serious, take this." She grabbed a napkin and pen from behind the bar and scribbled her number on it. "Here. Call me if you really decide to do this."

"Gotcha."

I strutted back to where Brooklyn sat and handed her the shot.

"Who was that?" she asked, once I was reseated.

"This girl I met earlier today at work."

"The fuck she want?"

"Tryna put me on, and I'm seriously considering it."

"Considering what? Being a stripper?" She burst out laughing. "Girl bye, you barely like getting dressed, let alone taking yo clothes *off* in front of strangers. The fuck you gone be in here doing? Dry humping these niggas with yo clothes on?"

"I'm serious Brook. Between having to borrow money from my Mom to pay my rent to pretty much getting my car taken in two days, I gotta do what I gotta do."

"Oh... you're serious?" Her smile faded once she looked into my eyes and knew I was serious.

"I'm tired of struggling Brook. I work and go to school every day! I try to live right. Do what I am supposed to do as a woman to get myself by. But then I look around at all these other women who are doing amazingly well just by having the right nigga, or stripping, or whatever they might be doing. It's just after awhile, you just wonder, when will my break come? Cause obviously, the right way aint the right way!"

"I hear what you saying NiNi, but you can't do that. Counting someone else's blessing or being envious of the next person's fortunes won't make you feel any better. Half these bitches out here flossing probably had to do some shit they aren't proud of just to get what they have. God is going to bless you when the time is right. Fast money is cool, but I can guarantee it'll come at a price."

"Right about now, I'll take that risk."

Chapter Four

"Why didn't you tell me you got into a fight young lady?"

"What are you talking about?" I responded, unsure how she would even know.

"Save it Germany. Cheyenne already called and told me what happened. What I want to know is, why didn't you tell me?"

"Nothing to tell. We fought and that's that."

"And you don't think that I, your mother, needed to know that you were out at a game in Oakland of all places, and got into a fight? Is that what you're telling me?"

"Pretty much ma. Just like Cheyenne didn't need to know." I said, rolling my eyes at the phone.

"What do you mean we didn't need to know?"

"Brooklyn didn't have to run back and tell her mama we got in a fight. We grown and we good. Nothing to talk about!"

"What's going on with you Germany? You haven't been acting like yourself lately."

"I'm just tired of struggling ma. I do everything I'm supposed to do as far as taking care of myself, and it's still not enough."

"I hear you baby, but in due time you'll figure it out."

"I have no time Mom. My car got repossessed last night so I'm really not in the mood."

"Why didn't you tell me you were behind on payments?" She huffed.

"So I could hear your mouth again about using my assets... Yeah, I'm good. But don't even worry ma, I'm taking your advice. I'm going to *Exquisete* today to see wassup."

"No the FUCK YOU NOT!" She was yelling at this point. "Lil girl who the fuck you think you talking too? Germany you grown, but don't get besides yourself. I'm not one of yo friends, nor am I one of them lil bitches you was fighting. I'll still fuck you up so check yourself!"

"Ma I gotta go! I'll talk to you later." I hung up and turned my phone completely off.

Don't nobody wanna hear that shit. She always talking about using my assets, and now I'm about too. Look what you created ma! I have arrived.

I arrived at *Exquisite* a little before five. It looked completely different during the day than it does at night.

"Mr. Nichols, you have someone here to see," the white receptionist said over the phone. "Go ahead, straight ahead to the right." She nodded to me.

"Thanks."

I was nervous as hell as I made my way to the office. Taking a deep breath, I knocked on the huge oak door twice.

"Enter!" Said the voice from the other end.

Strutting inside with as much confidence as I could muster, I took a seat at his desk.

"Hello Mr. Nichols, I'm Germany." I extended my hand and he left it dangling for a second before gracefully grabbing ahold of it.

"Miss Germany, you are absolutely breathtaking. Would you mind removing your glasses for me?"

I obliged him, as I shook the curls out of my face.

"Yes, you are definitely hired. You are going to bring so much new business in here. I can see it now."

"Money is the only motive." I added.

"When can you start and what will your stage name be?"

"I can start tonight, and Skyy. My middle name."

"It fits, you'll definitely have money raining from the sky."

We went over the legalities and shook hands in agreement.

I pray I didn't just sign my life over to the Devil.

Chapter Five

One Year Later

As I was preparing myself for my set, I took a deep breath. Sending a quick prayer up to God, I opened the curtains just as *Take my Time* by Chris Brown began to play. There was a full house inside *Exquisite* tonight. I began grinding my body to the beat of the music. I had on a pink see-through teddy, with my hair in loose curls around my face. The five inch clear heels on my feet only added to my sex appeal. As I was grinding to the floor, my hands went for my pot of gold. I held every man's attention as I put on a show. Bills of all denominations were flying onto the stage and I hadn't even removed my clothes yet.

The DJ mixed in Sammie's *Wetter*, and once I really got in the zone, it was on. I peeled off the straps to the teddy and freed my dark brown nipples. Climbing to the top of the pole, I began spiraling down, spread eagle. Cat-calls and whistles sounded throughout the upscale gentleman's club. Getting onto the ground, I crawled around on all fours, giving all these men an eye full of my kitty. Coming out of the teddy without missing a beat, I knew at least six of these niggas had cum in their pants. I enjoyed the attention I got from men. I craved it. Not having any consistent males in my life growing up, it was something that I had always yearned for. That's why I am the way I am. Stripping isn't something I necessarily enjoy doing, but it pays the bills, so it is what it is.

When *Fuck U All the Time* by Jeremih played, a man caught my attention. He was watching me closely, from the back of the club. He was so fine.

I got my eye on a target. He aint getting away tonight. Now that he was there, I knew I needed to be extra. Signaling the DJ, I had him play *Really Good* by Ty Dolla Sign and Joe Moses to give me a little bounce.

"Is the pussy really good?" One of the male patrons asked, singing along to the lyrics while also directing it as a question to me.

"It definitely is." I said, licking my lips at him.

Being a stripper was all about the fantasy, and to these men, that's exactly what I was. Every now and then if the nigga could afford to pay, I would play. If the money wasn't right, neither were the goodies. Turning my back to him, I turned my ass to the crowd and began making my ass cheeks jump. My ass cheeks were jumping like they had hydraulics as I dropped my left cheek, to make my right cheek jump.

"Man this hoe BADD!" Said the same patron.

Getting back on my feet, I was rolling my body to the drop of the beats. My eyes were staring directly at the mystery man, and his were staring directly into mine. Never losing eye contact, I put my right hand in my panties. Inserting two fingers into my dripping wet pussy, I pulled them out and began sucking on them. That was all I needed to do to have these niggas going crazy. *Always end a show with a bang.*

Picking up all my money, I went back into the locker room to cool myself off. Bitches of all nationalities worked at the club. None of these hoes liked me, and as they noticed all the earnings I made for the night, I noticed a few nasty glares from them. I gave them hoes no time as I put my money into my purse, grabbed my stuff and hit the shower.

Washing myself fast and thoroughly, I was in and out in five minutes. Grabbing a one piece zebra suit, I was on the floor. Bypassing numerous men who wanted a dance, I had eyes for only one person. Walking straight up to him as he sipped on his drink, I straddled him and went to work.

His drink was still in his hand as I put my best moves on him. He was a cool ass nigga I guess. He kept his hands to himself the entire time. My pussy was directly on his shaft, and when I felt the beast lying beneath his jeans awakening, I knew he was packing.

"You free tonight?" He asked, taking a sip from his glass.

Nigga hell yeah I'm free, I thought. I wasn't trying to seem overly juiced so I replied, "Could be."

"Well make it happen. We trying to get to know you," he flirted, looking from his dick to me.

"Let me get my shit and we can make that happen," I winked.

After I changed into some jeans and Ugg boots, I was following behind the mystery mans Range Rover in my newly purchased white Infiniti G37 coupe. I had been working at the club for a year, and everything about my lifestyle had upgraded.

When I followed him to the Four Seasons, I was quite impressed. *A nigga who don't mind spending a little money... I like*, I thought. He opened the door for me as the valet's took our cars for parking.

"What a gentleman." I acknowledged, as we walked into the lobby. I studied him from head to toe as he paid for our room. The way he carried himself and the way he walked. His swag was on a whole new level from the hood niggas I usually fucked with. After he paid for our room, we entered the elevator with little to no talking.

I was a little nervous when we entered the suite. He wasn't like any nigga I had ever dealt with and I wasn't sure how to approach this situation. I wasn't sure if I should just undress and go to work on him, or what. All these thoughts and different scenarios plagued me, and I knew then that I must really like him. Although I didn't actually know him, something about him drew me to him.

"You cool lil mama?" He was sitting on the bed staring at me.

"Yeah I'm good. Just a little tense from work," I lied.

"Come lay on the bed. Let me massage you. I got skills with these hands here," He smiled, that beautiful smile, holding his hands up in front of him.

"Yeah I'm sure you do." Lying down on my stomach, I felt him get on top of me.

"If you don't mind, can you remove your top. I need flesh on flesh contact."

I turned and looked at him and we started cracking up. "You hella funny," I blushed.

"I'll turn around and go get the lotion out the bathroom so you won't feel uncomfortable," he chuckled. Pulling off my shirt, I watched him as he entered the bathroom to grab the complimentary lotion off the countertop. When he came back, I was lying face down on the bed.

Drizzling the lotion on my back, I was surprised at the warmth of it. I was expecting it to be cold, and when he started rubbing it in while massaging my shoulders, I was in heaven.

He was gentle with me, and I loved it. No man had ever taken the time out to try and make me feel comfortable. All they wanted was to fuck.

Massaging me for about ten minutes straight, my nipples were hard as hell, and I was horny. I wanted to see what I felt beneath his jeans earlier so I turned over. "Let me do you now."

"You don't know how to massage," he challenged.

"Nigga please. You're not the only one who knows how to use their hands!" My nipples were staring directly at him, erect as hell.

"I guess I do have skills huh?" He smiled, staring at my nipples.

"Shut up boy. Hand me the lotion and take off that tank top." He did as he was told and lied on his back. "You want me to massage your front?"

"Yup." He was nodding his head up and down. I took in his beautiful physique and had to stop myself from skipping the foreplay and getting straight down to business. His entire upper half was covered in tattoos. The nigga held an eight pack, and was just an overall beautiful creature. His skin was flawless, and I was wet as hell.

Drizzling the lotion onto his body, I attempted to give him the best massage ever. I was sitting directly on his dick, and felt every little movement it made. My hands roamed all over his body as I attempted to give him a massage. With his eyes closed, I decided to make my move. I kissed him on his lips and that was the beginning to the beautiful night we were about to share.

He kissed me back and it was so passionate. I broke our kiss and started placing kisses all over his body. From the top of his head, to his nose, to his neck, to sucking on his nipples, to trailing my tongue down his chiseled stomach. I French kissed his belly button until I reached his jeans. I stared into his eyes as I began unbuttoning his Levi's. The black polo drawers he wore underneath were even sexy. Once I removed them and took in his nine inches, a devilish smirk appeared on his face.

"Cat got ya tongue?" He laughed.

"Nope. Its right here," I said, biting on my bottom lip. I grabbed his dick, and began circling the head with the tip of my tongue. I was skilled in the art of seduction and knew exactly what to do to turn a nigga out.

Taking the head into my mouth, I began sucking on it like a sucker. Slurping sounds reverberated around the room. His toes were curled as I took him all the way down my throat. The head of his big ass dick was boxing with my uvula causing me to almost throw up.

"Lil mama can't hang." He laughed, after I took him out of my mouth. I blushed with embarrassment after I got from my knees. Coming out of my jeans, I positioned myself on top of him. Right when I was about to slide down on his pole, he stopped me. "Hold on shawty. Latex is safe sex. I'm not tryna wake up with that *I'm late* text, so I gotta strap up."

Getting on the bed, I lied down on my back. I watched as he grabbed a magnum sized condom out of his pants, and I instantly got from the bed.

"Let me put that on you baby." I got from the bed and took the condom out of his hand. Pushing him to sit on the edge of the bed, I repositioned myself on my knees in between his lap.

Ripping the wrapper off the condom, I put it in my mouth and wrapped it around his dick using nothing but mouth. *No hands!* Once it was on, I sat on his lap and guided his thick dick into my dripping wet pussy.

Once I put as much as I could handle in, I went to work on that shit. I rode him so hard and it was the best fuck I ever had.

Stroking me from underneath, he took my nipples in his mouth. Sucking from the left to the right, we were both enjoying ourselves. When he turned me over on my back and put my left leg over his right shoulder, he had me. The headboard to the bed was banging on the wall and I knew the neighbors were getting an earful. He had my hair all disheveled as he beat my shit up. When I felt myself about to cum, I threw it back at him. "Right there! What the fuck is yo name?"

"Sincere," he moaned, getting ready to explode.

Tickling my clit as he continued to ram my pussy with all nine inches, I came and it was by far the best nut I'd ever bust. Shortly after, so did he. He lay on the side of me as we tried to catch our breath. I was in love. He was fine, paid, could fuck, and most importantly, could fund my lifestyle. He was definitely a keeper, and after tonight would become a permanent fixture in my life.

Chapter Six

Three Months Later

Turn You Out by Tyrese played softly in the background as I rode Sincere's dick. It was New Years Eve, and I needed my coins. I had his eyes rolling in the back of his head as he filled me up with his nine inches. No lie, my eyes were rolling in the back of my head as I felt my nut building. The bass of the song added to the passion that was built up between us. Sweat was dripping from Sincere's bald head, cascading down his chocolate ripped eight pack. His thumb was playing with my clit as I bounced up and down on his thick shaft.

"Damn girl! This shit good!" He moaned, just as I rose from his dick. Positioning myself onto my knees, I turned around so he could position himself behind me.

"Beat it up until you cum nigga." I ordered. His chocolate skin was glistening as he positioned himself behind me. Once the head was inside, I had to let go. My juices came squirting out and it was one of the best nuts I'd ever had.

"You good?" He asked, as I attempted to catch my breath.

It took me a few seconds to finally respond, before he slid back in. "Ooooowwww shit boy! Riight theeeerre!"

Sincere had stroke and as he pulled my silky curls, I felt myself about to cum again.

"You gon swallow this shit?"

My ass was pounding against his rock hard abs as I waited for the right opportunity to make him pull out and catch his nut. I was a certified freak, and swallowing was definitely on the menu. When I felt him about to bust, I turned around, ripped the condom off, and took him down my throat.

My head bobbed up and down as he lay straight on the bed. After about two minutes of my left hand playing with his balls while my mouth performed the best head I'm sure he's ever had, I had him cumming.

"Damn girl. You got the best brains in America."

"I know. I know." I acknowledged, after swallowing his kids. The salty taste went down sort of slow and I could taste it on my tongue. I handled it like a champ, and was on my way to the bathroom to brush my tongue.

Looking at myself in the mirror, all I could do was smile as I put some toothpaste on my toothbrush. I took in my 5'7" frame, thick thighs, light brown complexion, and black curls with newly installed peek-a-boo blonde highlights.

After I finished brushing my teeth, and gargling, I strutted with a model's precision back into the bedroom. Sincere's ass was knocked out in the bed, and I immediately went to work. Grabbing his Levi jeans off the floor, I pulled out a rubber banded stack of money and peeled off two thousand dollars. I knew it wasn't a lot but I knew he wouldn't notice the missing money. Putting the stack of money back in his pants exactly how I found it, I began to get dressed. Grabbing my lace panties off the floor, I put them back on. Dressing quickly, I was ready to hit the road. Clearing my throat, I attempted to get Sincere's attention. After trying several times and getting no reaction, I shook him until he awoke.

"Baby I'm about to leave."

"Why so soon?" He asked, rubbing sleep out of his eyes.

"I have a lot of stuff to do tonight and I need to go home and shower."

"Why not shower here? You got a toothbrush over here. I'm sure you done left a pair of panties over here that I've washed. Wassup?"

"Nigga you must have me mistaken with the next bitch. I aint never left no panties over here!"

"Shut the fuck up and don't start that shit!" He said, knowing I was about to get in his ass over the shit, but decided against it as my phone rang.

"Hello." I answered, turning my back on Sincere.

"Wassup bitch. We going out tonight, so be ready by ten." Brooklyn said, without giving me a chance to answer. Before I knew it, she had hung up.

"Sincere I'm going out tonight. I need some money to buy me something nice."

"How much you need?"

"How much do you think what we just did was worth?" I asked, putting my hands on my hips. I was in my ghetto girl 'nigga don't try me' stance as I watched him peel off two one-hundred dollar bills from his bankroll.

"There you go. And you thought I aint notice yo sneaky ass going through my jeans. Use the money yo ass thought you was stealing!"

Handing me the money, I snatched it and strutted right out the door without a backwards glance.

"You welcome!" He yelled, just before I slammed the door.

"What the fuck!" Was the first thing out of my mouth as I walked up on my white Infiniti G37 coupe.

Some hating ass hoe had keyed the word 'BITCH' across the passenger side door of my car. All I could do was laugh at the shit I went through with these hating ass bitches. Without a second glance, I hop in my car and was en route to my house to get my party on.

Drama and Haters was the furthest thing on my mind as I thought of what I was wearing tonight. Fuck the haters!

Chapter Seven

"Germany, Mommy is about to go have a conversation with Uncle Tony in her room. Please don't disturb us until I come out the room, you understand?"

I nodded my head up and down as I took a seat on the couch to watch an episode of Rugrats.

"You so fucking sexy." I heard him say to her as they shut the door to the bedroom.

As I watched Tommy, Chucky, Phil and Lil try to break out the playpen, I could hear the backboard to my Mom's bed begin to bang.

I turned the television louder as the sounds of her moans escaped her bedroom.

"Yes Tony, I want it!" she moaned.

"You want this dick?"

"Nigga I just said I did. Hurry the fuck up!"

They went on like that for the next twenty minutes. At the age of 10, I saw more than enough men come through that room to repeat the same conversation the last man just had with her.

I surfed through the cable channels once my episode ended.

"Uncle" Tony came waltzing out the room not too long afterwards.

"You gone be something so vicious when you get older," He whispered to me, licking his lips as he walked out the front door.

I locked the door and ran straight into my Mom's room. Cigarette smoke filled the air as she lied across her bed with nothing but a robe on.

I eyed the stack of money on her dresser as I took in her room.

"You see that money right there Germany?"

I nodded my head to answer yes.

"Being pretty was all it took for mama to get that money. If you say and do things men like, even if you don't want too, you can have

ANYTHING you want. When you get older, you'll understand the power of beauty and seduction."

I awoke out of my sleep in a cold sweat. I ran like a track star to the bathroom as I vomited all the contents of my stomach.

"Ugh, this shit is crazy," I whispered, wiping my mouth. I took a long look at my reflection in the mirror. I looked like the same female on the outside, minus the glasses, but I knew on the inside I was a completely different woman. I wasn't the same innocent young lady I used to be. I had become a *Seductress* looking for the biggest come-up.

Work by Omarion blasted out the speakers of *Exquisite* as Keyshia and I double teamed a patron on stage. She was dressed in a purple thong and black corset. A phony pony graced her head. Her body moved to the beat of the song amazingly as she danced behind the metal chair he was seated in.

I was dressed in nothing but black lace panties and thigh highs.

Slang by Rocko began to mix in. Keyshia escorted the male patron off the stage as my solo began. Grabbing the metal chair that had just been occupied, I spun it around and took a seat in it. Hands on my knees I began popping my ass to the beat of the song.

The sound of my ass smacking against the metal reverberated around the room.

"This hoe so mu'fucking bad!" I heard one of the niggas yell.

I Got That Sack by Yo Gotti started playing. I jumped into the splits, making money of all denominations rain onto the stage.

I was on all fours with my cat in this nigga face. *Left cheek, right cheek*. They were jumping like hydraulics. He smacked my ass with a stack of hundred dollar bills.

He rubbed the stack between his two hands as he rained it on me.

"Lil mama, you *it*!" He exclaimed.

Crawling over to him, I grabbed him by his beard and pulled his face to mine. *Light-skin nigga with cute features.* I stuck my tongue down his throat until he dropped his stack right on me.

"You right, I am *it*," I winked, closing my set.

Cat calls and whistles sounding throughout the club as I gathered my earnings off the stage.

Back in the locker room, I got my money together. I was so into it, I didn't even notice Keyshia walking over to me.

"Wassup girl!"

"Same shit, different night." I replied.

"You tryna make some extra money?" She quizzed, taking a seat next to me.

"Doing?"

"A party. That nigga you kissed during your set is throwing some shit at *Four Seasons*.

She began piquing my interest. "What they paying?"

"Five racks, plus whatever we make dancing."

"I'm with it!" I agreed, never turning down the bread.

"Okay, I'll see you there it starts in like *45* minutes."

"Cool," I responded.

An hour later I was pulling up to the hotel. After showering and grabbing a new costume to perform in, I was ready to get it popping.

The sounds of my heels *click clacking* on the floor could be heard throughout the lobby. Entering the elevator, I took it to the top floor and exited.

Stack of Ones by K. Camp greeted my ears as I walked to the door of the party. As soon as I was permitted inside, all eyes were on me.

I dropped the wheat colored Trench I sported, and walked straight to the middle of the floor where a dark-skin nigga was seated in a throne-like chair.

"Oh my God," escaped my mouth when I was directly in front of him.

We stared in each other's eyes for a split second before I got back into my zone.

From the Back by Kash Doll mixed in. I put my left leg over his right shoulder and made that ass drop. Herahm gripped my ass cheeks, spreading them open as his niggas made it rain on me. The custom made Chicago Bulls body suit and see-through *'come fuck me'* heels I had on left nothing to the imagination.

Turning around, I dropped into his lap. My head rested upon his shoulder as I grinded into his waist.

"I didn't even know this was you gorgeous," Herahm whispered in to my ear as I continued grinding into him.

"You never had the opportunity to know anything about me," I replied. Standing up, I grabbed the light-skin dude from the club and pushed him against the couch. Straddling him, I held the attention of everyone in that room. Including the other dancers.

Pulling down the left strap of the body suit, I did the same to the right. Freeing my nipples, I smothered ole boys face right into em. He took them both into his mouth.

"Ayyyyyyyyeeeeee!" The crowd yelled, as they threw the money.

Before I knew it, Herahm had snatched me up and shoved me into the bathroom.

"What the fuck you doing ma?" he asked, all in my face.

"Firstly, nigga you don't know me to be snatching me up like I'm yo bitch. Secondly, get yo mu'fucking hands off me!" I said, snatching my arm from him.

"My apologies ma, but I been searching for you since I met you at the game. There hasn't been a day that's gone by that I haven't thought of you. Shit probably sound like game, but I'm serious!"

"That's cute and all, but I'm on the clock bruh. I gotta go." I tried to walk pass him, but he was blocking my way.

"Nah fuck that. I been looking for you for the last two years! I'll be damned if I let you slip through my finger tips. As of tonight, you done stripping kuz you mine!"

I burst out laughing. "Really my nigga?"

"Yup, so what was you suppose to be making from this shit tonight kuz I'll throw it to you so we can get the fuck outta here."

"Ten racks," I lied, crossing my arms across my chest.

"Lying ass, this my congratulatory draft party. Wasn't nobody paying ten racks up in here." he laughed, pulling a wad of money out his pocket. He threw it to me, ordered me to grab my shit and we were gone.

Chapter Eight

"Germany, quit fucking playing with me! Where the fuck you been?" It had been two weeks since I last saw Sincere and I knew he was with the shit.

"Dude relax, I been taking care of my mama. But if you were really that concerned, you would have known that," I rolled my eyes.

He stood quiet for a minute until I brushed passed him and stormed up the stairs.

"Germany! Baby!" He yelled up the stairs.

Slamming the door behind me, I let my clothes fall as I strutted to the shower. Lathering up, I kept up my fake attitude as Sincere came waltzing his baldheaded ass into the bathroom.

He stood staring at me silently for what felt like an eternity before he said anything.

"Babe!"

I kept my back to him, acting as if I was really upset.

"Babe!" He repeated, aggression adding to his voice.

"Yup?" I replied, back still to him as I washed my hair.

"I love you."

"That's cool," I said, pushing his buttons.

"Germany, please don't start this shit. I'm sorry for assuming shit before actually checking to see what was going on. I'm sorry," he said, falling right into my trap.

Deciding to *forgive*, I opened up the shower door and yanked him inside by the neckline of his wife beater. The water drenched his wife beater, making it stick to his body. My hands roamed his boxers as he sucked on my neck. He had a grip on my hair, yanking my head back.

Spinning me around, he pushed my head down and slid inside me.

"Fuuuuuucck!" I moaned, feeling my knees quiver as he slid in and out of me.

"I feel you nigga!" I said through gritted teeth.

"You feel dat shit?" He moaned, smacking my right ass cheek.

"Yeah I do!"

Pulling himself out of me, he turned me around and lifted me up. Wrapping my hands around the shower head, he guided my legs onto his shoulders. Entering me, I let go!

"OOOOOOOOHHHHHHHH Shit! Fuck me!" I moaned, as I squirted my juices all over him.

He tickled my clit, as he slowly stroked me. "Who you got up in you Germany."

"Sinceeeeerrrreeee," I yelled, right as he pulled himself out of me and nutted on my stomach.

Letting go of the shower head, I grabbed a hold of his shaft and stroked it as the last drops of nut ran down the drain.

"That was good babe," I said, standing on my tippy toes to kiss his lips.

"I love you Germany."

Resting my back against his chest as he rinsed off, I closed my eyes as he held me. "You bet not ever give my pussy away, you understand?"

"Yes daddy," I replied, knowing less than five hours ago I had been popping my pussy on Herahm. A sly grin spread across my face as I thought of the session we just had.

If only these niggas knew, I thought, laughing to myself.

"What you doing tonight?" Sincere asked me, as he buttoned his suit.

"Not much of anything. Might go hang with my sister."

"Oh okay, well I got this meeting so I might be out late. I love you and I'll see you in a minute. I left some money on the dresser."

"How much?" I quizzed.

"Enough, that's all yo money hungry ass wanted." He said, smacking me on the ass as he walked out the door.

You damn right.

A white long-sleeve body suit and forest green mid-calf pencil skirt donned my body. Nude Jimmy Choo pumps on my feet. My hair was in a sleek ponytail, and diamond studs were in my ear. A nude clutch in my hands, and I was on my way to cash in. Not even a full three hours had passed since Sincere left the house and I was already on the hunt for nigga number 2.

"Name?" The bouncer asked, as I walked up to the front of the club.

"Germany-Skyy."

He scanned the list and once he came across the one and only, he stepped aside to allow me entrance.

The shit was packed.

"I wanna give my boy Herahm Santana a shout out for signing with the *Golden State Warriors*!"

The crowd showed mad love as applause erupted throughout the establishment. Scanning the crowd, my gaze locked in on Herahm.

Standing on the second floor dressed in a white custom made *Golden State Warriors* baseball jersey with his number on it, white jeans, that were razor cut at the knees and white Louboutins, this nigga looked Holy.

We hadn't locked eyes yet, so I mingled on the lower level until I needed to make my presence known.

"Damn you gorgeous," said a voice from behind me.

When I turned around, my heart dropped.

"Sincere!" I stuttered slightly.

"Look at you," he said, grabbing me by the waist. "I ain't ever seen you in this shit."

"Its new baby." I said, turning my body enough to see if Herahm had spotted me. His gaze was locked on to me like a hawk.

"I thought you had a meeting," I started, turning back to face Sincere.

"Shit wrapped early so I decided to slide through."

"That's interesting," I said rolling my eyes.

How the fuck am I about to get myself out this shit, I thought continuously.

Proud Side Nigga by DJ SpinKing blared out of the speakers.

The irony.

"Come dance with me baby," Sincere said, leading me to the dance floor.

"No Sincere," I said laughingly, following him to the dance floor.

"C'mon babe!" he yelled over the loud music.

I felt Herahm's eyes on me the entire way to the dance floor.

Guess I fucked that up with his mu'fucking ass, I thought.

Sincere held my hands as we danced in the middle of the floor. A huge grin was on his face as we danced.

I love you, he mouthed to me.

"I love you too, babe," I responded honestly.

I don't know why I do the hoe shit that I do because besides the bullshit, I know you might be the one. I just like the thrill of the game.

As we danced like eternal lovers in the middle of the floor, it felt for a moment that we were out there alone. Just the two of us, like nothing else in the world mattered.

That daze came crashing down, because the next thing I knew we were surrounded by security.

"Nigga get yo mu'fucking hands off me!" Sincere yelled, bucking at the security as they manhandled him towards the door.

I scanned the top floor to catch Herahm raising his glass to me as he cackled at the spectacle of Sincere's kick out.

The nigga had the nerve to pucker his lips at me as I turned my back to him to follow Sincere out the door.

"The fuck is this shit about?" he was yelling when I finally made it outside.

"Nothing personal sir, just following orders."

"Orders from who?" Sincere responded, fixing the jacket of his suit.

"Herahm Santana." He answered.

"Lil nigga who just got drafted to the *Warriors*?" he asked.

"Correct," responded the burly security guard.

"Say no More." He walked away with an agenda all over his face. "I'll see you at the house baby!"

Seated behind the wheel of my car, I headed home with tonight's events replaying in my head.

The text tone to my phone began playing, taking me out of my trance. Herahm's name flashed across my screen as I unlocked my phone to read the message.

Shit was cute how you pulled that lil stunt tonight, it read with the laughter emojis. *But say no more kuz I got a whole lot more games to play.*

A devilish smirk appeared across my face as I reread the message.

"This nigga right where I need em!" *my Seduction game is crazy!*

Chapter Nine

"You wanna go out for breakfast babe?" Sincere asked as I opened my eyes. He was sitting at the edge of the bed staring at the television screen with nothing but his white and green boxers on.

"Sorry pa, I'm supposed to be meeting with my Mother this morning for breakfast."

"It's good, I got some other shit to prepare for anyway." His whole demeanor changed after finishing his sentence.

"Like what?" I quizzed.

"Got some shit to handle stemming from that shit from last night."

"Let it go babe," I said, sitting up in the bed. "Just let it the fuck go, it's over and done with."

He stood from the bed and took a long stare at me.

"Fuck you mean let it go? The nigga clearly got beef with ya boy so I'm finna go see what's good."

"I guess," I responded, deciding to let it go. "Well I'm about to head home so I can get ready to meet my Mom."

"Aiight, I'll see you later?"

"I don't know."

"Here you go with this bullshit," he huffed, plopping his 6'3" ass on the bed.

Without responding, I dressed myself in the outfit I had on the night previously. "I'll see you later." Kissing him on the cheek, I exited the house.

Behind the wheel of my coupe, I racked my brain to figure out just how far I felt like Sincere was gone go with this Herahm shit.

So many different scenarios crossed my brain, that before I knew it, I had made it home. I ran straight to the shower and hopped in.

I washed thoroughly, and just as I was headed into my room wrapped in my cream colored towel, my phone rang.

"You got some nerve calling me after that bullshit you pulled last night." I said as soon as I answered the phone.

"Well good morning to you too beautiful. How yo morning going?" Herahm's sexy baritone greeted on the other end of the phone.

"Fine, what you want?"

"You." He responded bluntly.

"Well I'm not available!"

Click.

"This nigga got me oh so fucked up. Gone call after this shit, then I got this nigga on the hunt for his mu'fucking ass."

My phone rang again and I just let it rang.

"Fuck you nigga." I said, staring at the phone.

Once it started its third round of ringing, I finally budged.

"What?"

"Meet me tonight at my crib, I'll text you the address, just be there." *Click.*

This nigga hung up the phone, leaving me to ponder his invitation. *Nigga fuck off.*

I made it to breakfast right as my Mom was parking her car, but the surprise she had in tow with her was something I did not expect.

Olive-skinned, spiky black hair, and that wannabe-young outfit this man was wearing.

"Well hello Johnny," I greeted, calling my dad by his first name.

"Hey baby," he greeted back, crouching down to kiss my cheek as he took the seat to my left.

"What do I owe this pleasant surprise?" I asked, burning a hole in the side of my Mother's face.

"Well your Mother has told me that you haven't quite been yourself lately so-"

"And you came to do what? Because you don't know me to check on how I'm acting." I interrupted.

"I understand that Germany, but-"

"Aint no but nigga, you aint here, never been here, so continue to be gone. I've been living perfectly fine for the past 24 years just fine, so step the fuck off."

"You watch your mouth!" My Mother chimed in.

"And you!" I started, giving her my undivided attention. "Why would you bring him here as if he was gone do something? This nigga don't know me and if he would've been this concerned about me years ago, Tony would've never been able to touch me!" I yelled, snatching the black clutch I was carrying off the table and ran from the restaurant.

Tears fell from my eyes as I raced my car out of the vicinity of the restaurant. I was trying to get as far as possible, as quick as possible.

Calling Sincere as I headed to his house, I was greeted by his voicemail. Dialing back one more time, I got the same result.

"Oh my God Sincere! The one time I really need you, you aren't available!" I yelled.

My phone rang, and my heart jumped praying it was Sincere dialing back. A mug appeared on my face when I was greeted by the face of my Mother flashing on the screen.

Girl bye. I thought, turning my phone face down.

My text tone greeting me was the next thing I heard.

I hope she not texting me too!

Picking my iPhone 6+ off the passenger seat, I unlocked it to see who texted me. Surprisingly, I was greeted with the address to Herahm's house.

Bingo.

I uploaded his address to my GPS and headed straight there.

"Sincere, since you wanna play hoe games, two can play that game."

Chapter Ten

I pulled into his home located in the Hillsborough Heights-Brewer Subdivision neighborhood. I took in the tree-lined streets and huge estates.

"Damn this shit nice!" I complimented, as I made my way up the driveway to the house. There was a park-like garden in the front with a beautiful water fountain.

When I got to the huge cherry-wood doors, I used one of the two door knockers that had the initials *H* and *S* on them.

Conceited ass nigga, I thought.

"How may help you?" Said the Asian lady who opened the door, with her thick accent.

Removing my glasses from my face, I put on a smile. "Hi, I'm here to see Mr. Santana!"

"Mr. Santana expect you?"

I chuckled at her cute accent.

"Yes m'am."

"Ooookay, you come in, I get Mr. Santana."

I stepped inside the home and was blown away. I stood in the foyer of the immaculate estate decorated in all-white and was speechless.

White-gold chandeliers hung from the ceilings with diamond tear drops hanging from them. Beautiful artwork of African American culture hung perfectly on his walls leading down his hallway.

Just as I was really taking a good look around, my phone rang again.

"Mom stop calling me!" I whispered, pulling the phone out of my white Chanel purse.

"Well look who we have here!" A voice above me said, startling me just a bit. "And you wearing the same color as me," Herahm said, walking down the stairs.

I looked down at the white maxi dress I wore, completed with white Aldo sandals with a gold bow on the foot.

"Really?" I replied, looking him up and down. This nigga had on a pair of white Polo drawers, a white t-shirt with Burberry patches on his shoulders and some Nike socks.

"Am I not wearing white?" He asked, invading my space.

I could smell the Listerine on his breath as his mouth brushed against mine.

"Yeah you are," I said, taking a step back to take a good look at this nigga.

His chocolate skin was flawless. His gray eyes were to die for. Perfectly-lined white teeth. Standing at 6'4", nigga was fine. His usually faded hair had begun to grow out, leaving pretty curls atop his head.

Pulling me in close, he kissed me and all my troubles went away. It was so passionate, and when his hands caressed my neck as our tongues wrestled with each other, I felt the wall I began putting up against him fading.

"You hungry?" He asked, breaking our kiss.

Opening the mirror I had in my purse, I checked the *Kaoir* black lipstick I was wearing before replying, "where we going?"

He burst out laughing. "How you know a nigga wasn't gone cook for you?"

"Could you have been expecting me to be here at this time before you say things like that." I replied, cocking my head to the side.

He took a long stare at me before replying, "touché! Let me go throw on some jeans and we can dip. Feel free to look around."

"You know I was!" I laughed.

He ran up the stairs and I headed down the hallway. His grand living room and its high ceiling were beautiful. Taking my sandals off to let my feet sink into the white mink carpet, I felt as if I was walking on clouds. A white three-piece furniture set decorated the space.

Mink pillows with red accents sat upon the couches.

"You ready?" He scooped me from behind and kissed my neck.

"Who decorated your house?"

"I did."

"No seriously, who decorated this? You hired an interior decorator?"

"Real shit, I decorated every inch of this house sitting on these two acres.

"You have amazing taste, because this place is beautiful."

"Thanks gorgeous."

I blushed.

"You ready?" He asked, just gazing at me through those gray eyes.

"Mhmm. Lead the way Mr. Santana."

He flashed his pearly whites. Grabbing a hold of my hand, we walked into his four car garage.

"Which one you want to ride in?"

All of his cars were coke white-on-white.

Looking through his vehicles, I pointed to the 2016 Audi RS 7.

"Here." He handed me the keys and headed to the passenger side of the car.

"You want me to drive?"

"I didn't hand you the keys to take a picture for the *gram* with em." He laughed, hopping in the car.

"Cool." I got in the driver's seat and melted into the peanut butter leather. Putting my Chanel in the backseat, I opened the garage from the remote on the visor and backed the car out.

I connected my iPhone to his Bluetooth and went through my playlist.

Check by Meek Mill blared out the speakers in the car.

"Aye, this my joint! You don't know shit about that nigga Meek." Herahm said, nodding his head to the song.

"Boy bye!"

"These bitches fucking for a check check check check check check check!" He sang along.

If you only knew, I thought.

"Where we going to eat baby?" He asked, still bobbing his head to the music.

"I thought you had something in mind, I was just driving."

"So you have nothing in mind?"

A sly grin appeared on my face and I hit a U-turn in the middle of the street.

Vroooooom!

That car had power! I was flying down the street.

"Oh okay, I see you!" He laughed, turning the music down.

"I mean, you did hand me the keys!"

Five minutes later we were pulling up to *Sondra's*. One of my favorite restaurants since I was kid.

"I've never been here before and I been living in the city for four years."

"Well you been missing out," I responded, grabbing my Chanel from the backseat.

"C'mon gorgeous, a nigga is starving."

I blushed every time he complimented me. Something about him made me be able to just be that sweet little girl I used to be; before I fell victim to the game.

We walked inside the quaint establishment to an almost empty house. *Just the way I wanted.*

"Just the two?" asked the hostess.

"Yes, if it's possible could we get a spot on the other side of the restaurant?" I asked.

"I'm sorry but that side of the restaurant doesn't open until dinner time."

"I'll pay!" Herahm responded, pulling out his wallet.

"Um, I'll get the manager." She scurried to the back and I burst out laughing.

"Her young ass don't know what to do."

"Tell me about it." He responded, smacking me on the ass with his wallet.

"Boy bye!" I laughed.

The girl returned with her manager in tow.

"How you guys doing today?" Said the manager. Cute older lady with a short bob.

"We're fine, just was a requesting a little extra privacy." I responded.

"Well I'm sorry but-" she stopped midsentence once she took a long look at Herahm. "Wait a minute, aren't you Herahm Santana of the *Golden State Warriors*?"

"That's me m'am," he blushed.

"My son loves you! Follow me right this way." She grabbed a hold of his hand and led us to the other side of the restaurant.

I can definitely get used to shit like this. I thought, taking a seat in the booth.

"How much is it for being on this side of the restaurant?" He asked, looking at the manager.

"It's fine baby, all I ask is if you give me your autograph for my son, and a picture with me." She laughed.

I looked over the menu as *Mr. Hollywood* handled his business. My ass was starving and after jetting away from that set-up my mom called a breakfast date, I needed something in me.

"I'll give you guys a few minutes to look over the menu and then I'll be back to take your orders. Anything to drink in the meantime?"

"I'll take a mimosa." I responded, still looking through the menu.

"And for you?" She asked, turning her attention to Herahm.

"I'll take a water please."

"I'll be back."

She walked away, and I turned all my attention to Herahm.

"So *Mr. Hollywood*, let's talk." I said, laying my menu down on the table.

"About?" He responded, looking at me over the top of his menu.

"The birds and the bees. Nigga about everything, what the fuck." I laughed.

He started cracking up hysterically.

"What's funny?" I asked, missing a part of the joke.

"You."

"How so?"

Just as we were getting heavy into it, the manager returned with our drinks.

"Here you go," she said, putting our drinks down in front of us. "Are you ready to order, or you still need a little more time?"

"I'm ready. I'll take the egg-white omelet with diced ham and cheese and wheat toast on the side. Thanks." I ordered, handing her the menu.

"And for you sir?"

"I'll have the breakfast tacos on wheat tortillas. No cheese, light on the sausage and I want my eggs well done."

"It'll be out shortly." She grabbed his menu and went on her way.

"Back to where we were." I said, folding my hands underneath my chin, and looking his dead in the eyes.

"I just find it funny in the way you speak and carry yourself knowing in reality that isn't the real you."

"You could possibly know that how?"

"The day I met you in Oakland, I sort of got a feel for who you were. You don't trust people, you somewhat paranoid, and you really a good girl at heart."

"You got all of that from that one encounter?"

"I was intrigued. I watched how you carried yourself and I also watched as you turned every other nigga down. You're different."

I blushed.

"How old are you?" I asked.

"24, and you?"

"I'll be 25 in August."

"Got me a cougar," he laughed.

"Shut up," I chuckled.

"What's your ethnicity?" He asked, as the manager brought out our food.

"Vietnamese, Black, and Armenian." I answered, cutting into my omelet. "And you?"

"Hood and Dominican."

"So that's where the Santana comes in at. The Dominican side?"

"Yup. What's your favorite color?"

"Black," I replied. "Favorite food?"

"Chinese! What about you?"

"I love Chinese food!"

We spent the rest of the day just enjoying each other. Nothing sexual, organic chemistry; just brewing in the essence of lust.

Chapter Eleven

"Goodmorning my long-lost sister!" I greeted, kissing my sister on the cheek.

"Goodmorning you whore. I'm mad at you!" Brooklyn responded, smacking me on the ass as I took a seat across from her.

"Whyyyyy sis," I responded, putting my teal Hermes bag on the table.

"You and I used to talk about five times a day and now we talk maybe once a week."

"I'm sorry sis, but I have some good news so you can't be too mad at me."

"Me first!"

"Go!"

"I'm pregnant." She revealed, gushing.

Tears rushed to my eyes as I got up to give her a hug. "Oh my gosh Brooklyn. Really?"

"Yes, NiNi. I'm twelve weeks."

I reached down and ran my hands over the black maxi dress she wore, covering her belly.

"I'm so happy for you and Maurice!"

"Now it's your turn to spill the beans."

"I quit stripping and I been seeing Herahm."

"Bitch quit lying," she laughed, wiping the tears out of her eyes.

"I'm serious!"

"That's really good Germany, I'm so happy you back out of that environment, but what about this Herahm thing? What about Sincere?"

"He play too many games for me Brooklyn. It's just something about Herahm that I'm really attracted too."

"The money?"

"Bitch you trying it!"

"I hate to be the bearer of bad news sis, but Sincere been calling me. He said he hadn't heard from you since the other day when you went to breakfast with yo Mom so I told him I was meeting you here."

"Damn Brook," I said, rolling my eyes. "But it's whatever, if his ass show up I'll just deal with it."

"I had no idea. If you picked up the phone, I'd be included." She rolled her eyes playfully, and chucked a piece of ice at me.

"I love you sis, and I'm really happy for you. You told yo daddy?"

"No, besides Maurice, you the only other person... he did call me the day you guys seen each other though." Her voice faded off and she broke eye contact.

"And what he say?" I was nervously shifting in my seat, because this topic had never been discussed with anyone.

"He said something about a guy named Tony. He was crying and yelling about how angry he was and how he should have been there for us."

I took a deep breath.

"You don't have to talk about it Germany. Not until you're ready."

"Thanks sis, I love you."

"And I love you back." Her eyes shifted pass me and I followed her gaze.

"Wassup Brooklyn, and hello stranger!" greeted Sincere, dressed like he was headed to a funeral.

"Hi," we both said dryly.

"Sis you gone be good?" Brooklyn asked, eyeing Sincere.

"I'll be straight, gone and head out and I'll call you later."

Kissing me on the cheek, she brushed pass Sincere and headed to her car.

"So what's good Germany? Niggas aint heard from you in a few days."

"And?" I responded, crossing my arms across my chest.

He spun a chair around and sat in it.

"You don't feel like you owe me an explanation as to where the FUCK YOU BEEN?"

"Nah, I don't. Because when I needed yo baldheaded ass you was nowhere to be found, so I don't even wanna hear no bullshit from yo ass." I snatched my purse off the table and stormed out.

"GET YO ASS OVER HERE!" He yelled, making a scene.

"WHAT!" I yelled, spinning on my heels.

"Germany, who you fucking?"

That caught me off guard.

"Excuse me?"

"Hoe you heard what the fuck I said?"

I laughed in this nigga face.

"So I'm a hoe now? That's cool, kuz I'm a hoe who done traded her old nigga in for one with much more coin. You might know e'm, the nigga did have you thrown out the club... bitch!"

Smack!

The devil must've jumped in this nigga, because what I saw behind his gaze was nothing to be taken lightly.

"So it's like that Germany? I got you ma, you and that nigga, don't even trip."

I held on to my face as I watched him walked out of the establishment and hopefully my life.

"Are you okay Miss? We've already called the police!" Said an older white lady, walking towards me with her phone to her ear.

"I'm fine," I replied holding back my tears.

I ran to my car and drove off. The tears fell as I rubbed the spot where Sincere had smacked me.

When you were thirteen you made a pact to yourself that no other man would ever put there hands on you and Sincere is no exception. He gotta get it! Plots and schemes plagued me as I headed straight to Herahm's house.

Sincere, it's on!

Chapter Twelve

"How'd the meeting go with your sister?" Herahm asked, opening the door.

I fell into his arms and began to plant the seed.

"What's wrong Germany?" He asked, pulling my face up.

His whole face flushed. "What happened to your face?"

"Sincere showed up to breakfast with my sister and I and things got out of hand." I dug face into his chest crying.

"I'm gone handle that nigga! On everything I love, that nigga dead." He declared.

"No Herahm. You just made it to the NBA, you don't need to get caught up in any scandals. It's fine!"

"Nah fuck that. You my bitch, I'll be damned if niggas out here disrespecting my woman."

I was smiling so big on the inside.

"I wanna help," I revealed, leaving him speechless.

"What you mean you wanna help?"

"I'm gonna set him up and we can take him out. This nigga smacked me in my face, I got to get him back."

"You sure?" He asked, looking at me with concern.

"Yes Herahm and I know exactly how I'm gone do it."

"Spill."

"I'll somehow get Herahm to a hotel to try to smooth things over. Get em drunk or some shit and once he let his guard down, you handle it."

"When we doing this shit? Kuz I got some press shit in LA I got to handle by next week."

"Tomorrow."

"Get it done."

Chapter Thirteen

"What happened after I left yesterday?" Brooklyn asked from the other end of the phone.

"Girl, Sincere came in there acting a mu'fucking fool. Yelling and carrying on."

"Oowee. That nigga a trip." She laughed.

"But can you do me a favor, kuz the bitch aint answering my phone calls."

"Wassup?"

"Text him and tell him I said to meet me at *Club Leola's* tonight by nine."

"I got you."

"How my little snuggle butt doing in that oven?" I laughed, thinking about the bundle of joy my sis was carrying.

"Fine I guess," she laughed. "I'm ready to find out what I'm having though."

"Is that Germany baby?" I heard Maurice ask through the phone.

"Yes it ME BRUHTHERRRR," I yelled.

They started cracking up.

"Yo ratchet ass," Brooklyn said, still chuckling.

"Just a lil bit. Girl I gotta go, Herahm just walked through the door, but please do that for me ASAP."

Click.

"She gone do it?" He asked after I hung up.

Nodding my head up and down, I took a deep breath knowing once I entered this aspect of the game, I couldn't turn back.

"What time is your hair appointment?"

"Tanaya said she'll be here to do it by four."

"Oh okay coo. Is that who normally do your hair?"

"Yup, she been doing me and Brooklyn hair for years."

"Keep her, cause she be having you hooked." He laughed.

"Shut up. I'm about to go get my nails done."

"How long you think you gone be?"

"Couple hours. You need something?"

"Nah I'm straight. Just be back at a decent time, you got one last final for school."

Fuck I forgot all about that.

"Right, you did forget," he said, reading my mind.

"I'm going to get it done."

I strutted to my car wearing black jeans and a black tank top. Gold *Giuseppes* on my feet with my hair in a tight bun. Black *Raybands* on my face and gold studs in my ear.

Checking my lipstick in the mirror once I hopped in, after giving myself the once over I was good to go.

Desiree's Nail Bar was a new establishment in San Francisco that I had been hearing great reviews about.

Located off Embarcadero, I was there in no time.

"Welcome to *Desiree's Nail Bar*," said the receptionist when I walked inside.

"Hello." I greeted back, taking my shades off.

"What can I do for you today?"

"I need a full-set, pedicure, and my eyebrows done."

"Okay, have a seat right there and I'll see whose available."

I took a seat and looked around the place. Decorated in white and black, it was a cute place. Black and white photos of Dorothy Dandridge and Marilyn Monroe hung throughout the establishment.

"Yes bitch, he was asking me to go to them stupid ass meeting but I wasn't feeling that shit.

Fake ass Basketball Wives." I overheard a female getting her feet done say to her friend.

"I've been to a couple," Said the brown skin chick with the kinky curls sitting next to her.

"All I know is his black ass getting on my nerves with the discreet bullshit. It's like he use me as a convenience."

Her conversation definitely piqued my interests, but before I could really get in her mouth, the receptionist returned asking me to follow her.

I looked the bitch up and down as I walked pass her to get to the station the receptionist was directing me to.

Light skin chick with curly hair and freckles. Brown eyes with dimples.

"That Aldo bag you rocking is cute." I laughed, putting my newly purchased gold Berkin bag on my shoulder as I took a seat in the chair.

I looked over my shoulder to catch the bitch and her friend whispering something about me. *Bitch try it if you want too*, I thought, keeping aware of my surroundings.

Turning my attention to the television, of course I see my face.

Herahm Santana, of the *Golden State Warriors*, girlfriend is alleged stripper Germany-Skyy. Photos of me flashed across the TV and I caught the bitches ice grilling me.

The text tone of my phone went off.

I'll be there, the message from Sincere read.

"And the games will begin!" I said aloud, reading the message again.

Chapter Fourteen

"Baby? You know you looked good at the club tonight?" Sincere complimented, as he pulled me into his embrace.

"Thanks baby. After spending four hours getting dolled up for yo ass, I better look good!"

"Is that right?" He asked, licking his lips.

"Yeah." I acknowledged as I unbuttoned the jean shirt I wore.

"So how you gonna show me your appreciation for giving you a second chance after you pulled that hoe shit?" Sincere asked, watching me wiggle out my skirt. Pulling away from Sincere, I strutted toward the King-sized bed in the middle of the hotel room. Gazing in the mirror that was on the ceiling positioned directly above the bed, I watched his manhood begin to rise as he lusted after my body.

"Baby, you so fucking sexy" Sincere stated somewhat slurring his words.

"I know," I replied, nibbling on his ear.

"I want some." Watching Sincere as he pulled off the jeans he wore, I knew it was almost time to execute my plan. *The nigga really think shit was sweet after he put his hands on me.*

As he pulled his jeans off, I started caressing his manhood. I licked him from his chiseled stomach up to his earlobe.

Standing from the bed, I looked into his eyes. Grabbing ahold of that dick, I began to jerk him off. Grabbing my right nipple, he began tracing his finger around it.

"Damn baby. You got me on brick," he whispered as his eyes began to roll in the back of his head. Picking me up off the bed before I could react, he began lowering me onto his throbbing dick.

"Wait baby! I gotta go to the bathroom, and I know you better have a condom," I stalled, making him lower me back onto the bed. Sincere's gaze followed my ass the entire way to the bathroom.

Once I locked myself in the bathroom, I turned on the light and took a deep breath. Looking in the mirror, the shower curtain moved a little.

Walking toward it, I slid it back just enough to see Herahm holding his hands to his mouth to silence me.

"You okay?" He mouthed to me through the mouth opening of the mask he wore.

Nodding my head up and down, I reclosed the curtain.

"Everything alright in there?" Sincere yelled from the other side of the door.

"Yeah, I'm coming out now." I took another deep breath and exited the bathroom, leaving it open.

Dropping to the floor, I began crawling toward him. Coming out of my panties without missing a beat, I kept my eyes locked on his. Reaching the bed, I came up with nothing on but my red bottom stilettos.

"Dance for me baby," he said as he rubbed the head of his dick. Turning on his iPod, *Seduction* by Usher began to play out of the speakers in the ceiling. Walking to the middle of the floor, I put on a show. Closing my eyes I began moving seductively to the music.

Imagining I was back in the club, all emotions left my body. *It's a job, just like any other patron in the club,* I tried to convince myself.

Getting on my knees in front of him, I circled my tongue around the head of his dick. Feeling his dick beginning to pre cum, I slurped it like left over drool.

"I got something for you," he stated in a strained voice as he pushed me on my back. He headed to the edge of the bed and pulled me close by my legs.

"Turn the lights off!" I said, before he tried to eat the cookies.

He did as he was told and turned the lights off.

Downtown by SWV began playing just as he got on his knees in between my legs. His tongue flicked against my clit, and although I hated his guts, the shit felt amazing.

Moving his tongue lower, he entered my flood gates. I gripped his head as he tongue fucked my pussy.

I was running from that head game. His hands were wrapped around my waist, keeping me in place.

"FUUUUUUUCK!" I moaned, unable to fake it any longer.

"That nigga you been fucking do this shit to you?"

I could faintly hear the sounds of the curtains in the bathroom move and I knew it was almost time.

"C'mon Sincere!"I said, getting back in character.

Just as he positioned himself to get on top of me, he never saw it coming.

Boom Boom Boom, rang out as Herahm let off three shots into the dark. A loud thud of his body hit the ground and I was shook.

"Oh my gosh," I whispered, trembling.

Herahm grabbed me by hand and sprang into action. Grabbing the wigs and dresses he had in the bag that was stashed underneath the bed, he began changing.

Coming out of the fear, I followed suit. Not even a minute had passed before both of us were in disguise. In full on drag, Herahm complete with dress, wig, shades and kitten heels was ready to go.

Dressed in a hoodie, baseball cap, and sweats, I on the other hand looked like a young boy.

We exited the hotel room and made our way to the emergency exit. My nerves were shot as I inched closer to the fire alarm I had to pull.

Ring Ring Ring Ring Ring rang out, as the guest came fleeing out of their rooms. We along with everyone us on our floor ran down the stairs as the hotel staff filed everyone out.

Safely in our car, we made a quick exit. The flashing of red and blue got closer to us as squad cars raced to the hotel we were fleeing. Driving as casually as possible, we attempted to not draw any unnecessary attention to ourselves.

It's all over Germany, I repeated to myself as a single tear slid down my face. *It's all over.*

Chapter Fifteen

It's been a month since the incident with Sincere happened and things had started going back to normal. No news about Sincere and the hotel had been reported so I just assumed shit was straight. Herahm and I were damn near inseparable and it was total bliss.

"Babe!" he called from upstairs as I painted my nails on the couch.

"What?"

"You want to go to a movie premiere in LA?"

"Duh."

I got from the couch walking on the back of heels to head upstairs.

"What movie is it?"

"*Gangsta' Bitch*, based on the novel by Bronchey Battle."

"I read that book, I would love to go to the premiere."

"Ok, the jet will be at the airstrip by six so just be ready. I'll buy you something to wear and all that good shit when we get out there. Is that fine?"

"Buying me new shit is always fine," I laughed.

"Go pack whatever you feel like you gone need because we leaving here in less than a hour." He said.

Still walking on my heels, I went and grabbed the spare Louis Vuitton luggage set he had in the closet and started throwing miscellaneous shit inside it.

"Babe?"

"Yes?" I answered.

"Have you ever went on a trip anywhere?"

"No." I revealed.

"I can tell," he laughed, leaving me a little embarrassed. "It's fine babe, Miss Kim will do it for you."

"Fine. I'm gonna go shower and then I'll be ready to go. My feet are probably gone get fucked up so prepare to get me a pedicure when we touch down."

"Yeah yeah, just hurry up."

My clothes dropped where I stood as I made my way into the bathroom and hopped in the shower. Lathering my towel with soap, I closed my eyes and let the water cascade down my body.

My sixth sense kicked in, because when I opened my eyes, Herahm was standing in front of the shower.

Opening the shower door, I pulled him inside and removed all his clothing. My hands roamed his drawers until his dick was rock hard.

Getting on my knees, I decided to put in some work. Circling the head of his dick with the tip of my tongue, I looked at Herahm to see the pleasure on his face. Only taking the head into my mouth, I sucked on it, slurping sounds reverberating around the shower.

Sliding it inch by inch into my mouth, I cupped his balls in my left hand as I took as much as I could down my throat. His hands were playing in my hair as I gave a Superhead worthy performance. Taking him out of my mouth, I licked from the vein on the back of his thick dick down to the base, and back up again. Ten minutes of me deep-throating passed, before I got off my knees and slid down on his pole. My opening was so wet for him. Our tongues were making love with each-other. Gripping me by ponytail, he pulled my head back to lick and plant sweet kisses down my neck.

"Oh shit baby, this shit feels so goooooooood!" I moaned. Our sweet love turned into a fierce fuck as he began ramming his dick in me.

Turning me around, he sat down on the built in seat in the shower and I got on top of him. Sweat had formed on his brow as he lifted me up and down on his dick. I was in pure ecstasy.

My love coated his dick as he brought me to an orgasm. My body was shuddering as my heart rate sped up. "Oh my GOOOOOOOD! Yes, baby, YES!" Herahm wasn't a stingy lover. He made sure to satisfy me every time before he caught his nut. He shot his load inside me, and we both collapsed.

"That was good babe." I said, now washing myself again.

"I know, now speed up it up a little because we gotta go."

We touched down in LA a little before *8:00pm*. The Penthouse Suite inside *The Beverly Wilshire* was exquisite. Panoramic views from the spacious terrace. Taking a step back inside, I walked into the media room with the 60-inch flat screen.

"Babe come check out the kitchen!" He called to me.

The dining table for 10, was made entirely glass. Even the chairs!

"I'm going to check out the master."

An expansive walk-in closet and ensuite bathroom with sleek glass tiles, exotic stones and marble, with an oversized shower and deep-soaking tub. *Damn!*

"I know you gone like this part." He said, walking out the closet. "Penthouse are treated to Ferrago amenities, five hours of personal time, including a choice of spa, trainer, fashion stylist or hair and make-up artist, a dedicated personal concierge daily, daily use of a luxury car and a refrigerator stocked weekly with guests' favorite food items." He read off the brochure.

"Oh yeah, I love it here."

He wrapped his arms around me and just stared into my eyes. So much care and love shined through his gaze.

All I could do was blush as we rocked side to side.

"What time is the premiere?"

"Ten."

"Herahm it's already 8:20." I replied, looking down at the rolex on my wrist.

"And your dress and make-up artist will be here by 8:30, now go take a shower so we can be on time."

"You cease to amaze me Herahm Santana."

"I'm sure I do, Germany-Skyy." He kissed on me the lips and sent me on my way.

This shit is really crazy that this nigga got me open like this. Only been messing around for a little under four months and I'm hooked. It's not the money that has me, its... it's the sense of security you feel after everything you've been through. This might just be the one. I was so deep into the conversation I was holding with myself I didn't even hear Herahm yelling for me to get out the shower."

Strutting into the living-room with the hotel supplied robe on. My hair was wrapped in a towel, and Ferragamo slippers on my feet.

"Hello," the make-up artist greeted when I took a seat in the chair.

"How are you?" I greeted back. She was a cute brown skin chick with a long weave parted down the middle.

"Girl, I'm good." She laughed.

"I love your hair!"

"Thank you, I did it myself."

For the next hour, I sat up getting pampered. Herahm spared no expense, from pedicurist to a stylist, and everything. Had everything planned out, just assuming I'd accompany him on the trip.

He had a limo ready for us by 9:30, and once I was seated inside the stretch benz, I exhaled.

"You nervous baby?" Herahm asked me, licking his lips at me in my one of a kind dress.

"Yes, I just haven't ever been to anything like this."

"You look amazing baby, you'll be fine."

The limo pulled up to the red carpet 45 minutes later, and I sent up a quick prayer to God that I wouldn't fall in my dress as the driver opened up the door.

The paparazzi, media and fans started screaming, "Herahm, over here! We love you Herahm, you are the next Michael Jordan! Smile that million dollar smile right here."

"Oh, so I'm in the company of the next Michael Jordan?" I joked, nudging him.

"Yeah, I'm something like greatness." He laughed.

"Well shit, when them new Santana 11's gone drop?"

We both cracked up.

"That looks like love right there!" One of the reporters yelled out.

We walked down the red carpet hand in hand and when Kelly Osbourne came over to interview me and ask who I was wearing, I knew shit was real.

"Well hello beautiful. Who are you wearing tonight?" she asked, in her British accent.

"I am wearing an up-and-coming designer by the name of Angel Burks. I took a step into the glam cam so that everyone could marvel over my dress. It was a white lace mermaid style dress with a lace draping at my waist. The black leotard underneath fit my body like a glove and when she told me she was nominating me for a best dressed award, all I could do was smile. I noticed Nicki Minaj standing over there in her red dress, I was unsure of the designer, but that bitch was bad. She didn't have shit on me though, and when she came over and complimented me and asked if she could take a picture, I knew Angel's dress was really the shit! So many people complimented me on the red carpet, but when Idris Elba did, I almost died.

It seemed as if Herahm did a million interviews as we made our way down the carpet. Answering who I was for the umpteenth time, we were finally seated.

I really enjoyed watching the movie. *Gangsta' Bitch* stayed true to the book and it was amazing seeing it acted out.

Herahm and I laughed throughout the show and were really enjoying each-others company. I was introduced to so many stars and asked frequently was I an actress or model, and it was all so flattering. None of these mu'fuckas in here would've ever been able to guess I was a high-class prostitute fucking a Hermes bag. The shit was crazy. Once the show was over, we left the Staple Center and enjoyed each-other physically in the back of the limo all the way back to the hotel.

Chapter Sixteen

"Germany, I'm about to run to the store real quick. Tony is on his way over here, so when he comes, open the door. If it's not him, don't open that door. Do you understand?"

"Why can't he come once you get back?"

"Girl just do what I said!"

Watching her walk out the door, I dreaded it. I prayed that he didn't make it before she got back because being alone with him was the last thing I wanted.

Going in my room, I turned my stereo on full blast to drown out any sounds of a knocking door. Destiny's Child was pumping through the speakers.

Knock Knock, I faintly heard over the music.

I ignored it, turning the music a little louder.

The house phone ringing, diverted my attention.

"Hello?" I answered, turning the stereo down."

"Go open the front door Germany, Tony said he been out there knocking on the door!" My mom yelled from the other end of the phone.

Rolling my eyes, I hung up the phone and walked to the front door. Goose bumps ran up arm as I turned the door knob.

"Wassup Germany." He grinned that perverted grin.

Waving, I made my way back into my room and locked the door.

Please hurry home Mom, I whispered to myself.

Taking a seat on my bed, I watched his shadow walk pass my room.

Hurry up Mom!

Knock Knock.

"What?" I yelled to the other side of the door.

"What are you doing?" He asked.

"Nothing."

"Can you open the door?"

Taking a deep breath, I walked over to the door and opened it.

"What?"

"What you in there doing?"

"Nothing."

"Open this door," He ordered, bombarding his way into my room. "Yo mama told me about them boys you been talking too, you hiding one up in here?"

"I don't even like boys so get out of my room."

I tried pushing him out of my room but he rushed me to the bed and pinned me down.

"You so fucking sexy." He whispered in my ear while keeping a firm grasp on my wrist.

"Get off me," I bucked, trying to get him off of me.

He started planting kisses on my neck, and with everything in me, I screamed at the top of my lungs.

"Shut the FUCK UP!" He yelled, cupping his hand around my mouth.

I bit down as hard as I could into his hand.

"Bitch!" He yelled, ripping his hand away from me.

He ripped at the button on my jeans as I sent a silent prayer up to God to take me out of my misery. Tears were streaming down my face and all I could do was keep fighting.

"Stop it!" I yelled.

"If you give me what I want all this will go away Germany!"

I kept fighting him and fighting him until my Mom's words popped into my head.

"If you say and do things men like, even if you don't want too, you can have ANYTHING you want."

Something inside me clicked, and I immediately stopped fighting.

"You want this pussy?" I asked him, mimicking the things I've overheard my Mother say for years. At thirteen years old, I had been around more than enough adults to know what Tony was after.

"Oh, now you want to act right?"

"Get on your back and find out."

On the inside I was shitting bricks, but the fighter in me was willing to say anything to get this nigga up off me.

He obliged me and lied straight on his back in my twin sized bed. Wrestling his jeans off, he licked his lips at me as I crawled toward the bed.

He pulled his penis out and I almost vomited all the contents of my stomach. Oh my gosh this is disgusting.

"Put your mouth on it." He ordered.

I did exactly as I was told and bit down as hard as I could into the flesh.

He screamed in agony and I ran straight out the front door.

"HELP ME! HE'S TRYING TO RAPE ME!" I yelled as soon as I got outside.

"What's wrong?" Yelled Miss Janet, the black lady who lived next door to us."

"He tried to rape me," I cried as she ran over to cradle me.

"DALONTE! ANTHONY!" she yelled calling for her two sons. They came running out, looking like they were ready to kill somebody.

"Wassup ma?"

Just as they walked up, Tony came running out the apartment towards me.

"Bitch im gone kill you!" He yelled.

"Beat his motha fucking ass!" she ordered, shielding me from Tony.

Her two sons rushed Tony and it was on. They pummeled him and by time my Mom made it back, the police had arrived as well.

It took two officers to restrain Miss Janet from jumping on my Mom.

"You stupid bitch, how the fuck you gone leave her in the house with this nigga?" She yelled.

"What happened?" My Mom asked, looking around at the commotion. Red and blue lights were flashing in front of our house as all the neighbors gathered around being nosy.

"He tried to rape yo daughter you stupid bitch!"

Chapter Seventeen

I woke up in a cold sweat panting heavily. Tears formed in my eyes, and I had to control my breathing.

Reaching for the bedside table, Herahm sat up and looked at me.

"What's wrong babe? What's wrong?" He cradled me as I just wept in his arms.

The nightmare of my past was haunting me and I didn't know what to do.

"You okay?"

"Please don't ever hurt me Herahm. Whether it's physical or emotional. If you aren't ready to commit to just me, please tell me. I'd rather know what I'm dealing with then to be blind in a pretend fairytale." I wiped the tears out of my eyes as I let Herahm in my heart.

"Germany, ever since I met the cute girl in the hoodie and Timbs at the park; I was hooked.

Something about you, I needed. When I told you I thought of you every day I wasn't playing. You are mine!"

He kissed me so passionately and we made love right there in the moon light.

Chapter Eighteen

The sun shined brightly through the curtains on the windows. Herahm and I had been practically inseparable for the past month and I hadn't ever been happier. After the premiere we made it official and I never turned back. Our relationship was amazing and all the perks of being with a star athlete didn't hurt.

"Goodmorning baby," Herahm greeted, kissing me on the forehead.

"Goodmorning daddy."

"I'm hungry. Can I have some waffles please?"

"You sure can. With chocolate chips?"

"Sure big baby."

Herahm, removing the covers looked down at his dick. His soldier was standing at attention, and I knew it was about to go down.

Spitting on the head of his dick, I took as much of him down my throat as possible. Pulling my panties to the side, I got on top of him and let him slide in. My pussy was shaped to the curve of his dick, and I felt every inch sliding inside me. As I rode him slow, he began to kiss me so passionately. Our tongues were making love with each-other. His hands were intertwined in my mane. Pulling my head back he nibbled on my neck ferociously.

"Who pussy is this?" He asked, smacking me on the ass.

"Yours daddy, its YOURSS!" I screamed.

"This shit wet babe!" He moaned. Our session was non-stop fucking as my ass bounced on his abs. Turning me around, he got on his knees and stuck his tongue in my pussy.

"Heraaaaaahm!" I moaned, letting my love coat his tongue.

He lapped it up and he continued licking my opening. His left thumb was playing with my clit, and I felt myself about to bust again.

"Put it back in Herahm!" I moaned, wanting to feel him back inside of me.

"What you want?" He asked, still licking me.

"I wanna feel daddy dick!"

"You want daddy dick?"

Nodding my head up and down, he obliged me. Pinning me against the wall, he cuffed my left leg and reentered me.

The steam from the shower made it even more sexy. He was stroking my love box. I was in pure ecstasy. My love coated his dick as he brought me to another orgasm. My body was shuddering as he continued stroking me. "YESSSSSS! Yes, baby, YES!"

He shot his load inside me, and we both panting. I lied my head on his chest while trying to labor my breathing.

Hopping out of the shower an hour later, I went inside my walk-in closet, to find an outfit for the day. I was headed to go meet up with some of the other player's girlfriends and wives. I put on a pair of black high waist pants, white tank top tucked inside, with a hot pink blazer on top. The cheetah print pumps herahm had picked up for me with spikes on the toe was the finishing touch to my ensemble.

"Where you going baby?" He asked, watching me put my blush on the mirror.

"I'm about to go meet up with some of the other player's girls."

"Ok cool, I'm about to head off to practice. Thank you for taking the initiative to become to help me out. You being a part of the organization is a good look."

"It's fine babe, I don't mind the *Saber* Wives," I laughed, thinking of the hit show *The Game*.

Catching on, he started cracking up.

"Let me know if you see Tasha and Kelly. I gotta go babe." He laughed, kissing me on the cheek and walking out the door.

Behind the wheel of the white Ferrari Herahm always drove, I headed to the hotel they were holding the meeting at.

Dipping in and out of lanes, I looked in my rearview mirror to catch a black Volkswagen Jetta trying to keep up with me. Hopping off the freeway, I watched the car do the same.

"What the fuck is this shit?"

I kept a close watch on the car as I pulled up to the hotel. Hopping out the car, I walked straight towards the Jetta that was sitting across the street.

"What the fuck!" I yelled, as I approached the vehicle.

The sounds of screeching tires could be heard as the car peeled off. The fuck was that about, I thought, making a mental check to tell Herahm about this.

"You okay girl?" Asked, one of the girlfriends as I headed back towards the hotel.

"Yeah, some creep following me."

"Oh hell no. Let's go," she said, walking behind me as we entered the hotel.

"I'm Germany," I said, extending my hand to her.

"I'm Karen." Standing at 5'5", dark skin with huge kinky curls, she was absolutely stunning. Perfect white teeth and high cheek bones.

"You are gorgeous," I complimented.

She started blushing. "Well thank you and so are you. And I love the shoes." She complimented back.

We walked into the ballroom where the meeting was being held.

"Hello ladies." We said in unison as we took a seat in the white chairs that sat in the middle of the room. Different shades of purple and gold was the theme.

The feel of my phone vibrating in my purse caught my attention.

Sliding it out of my bag, I answered it as discreetly as possible. "Yes babe," I answered.

"How's it going?" He asked.

"Fine, it's actually just about to start."

"Okay, well tonight we going to *Club Leola's*."

"*Club Leola's*?" I repeated, unsure if I heard right.

"Yeah, I had something sent to the house for you to wear already."

"Okay babe."

Click.

"Ya boo?" Karen asked me as I put my phone back in my purse.

"Yeah." I giggled, swiping my bang out my eye.

"Welcome ladies, I want to thank you all for showing up today!" Said Jahmila Connors, wife to small forward Jamie Kahn. "I'm gonna get right down to business. Us, the wives and girlfriends are the backbone to the team. And as the counterpart to these men, we are responsible for certain things to get our men where we need them to be."

Jahmila spent the next hour going over rules and protocols of "the game." I swear I was a part of an episode of the show.

Herahm and I pulled up to the house at the exact same time.

"Aye lil mama, you looking cute behind the wheel of that Ferrari." He called out to me, from his white 2016 Jeep Wrangler on 28" black rims.

"I know; it's my boyfriend's." I replied.

He grinned and hopped out the car with his gym bag in tow.

"How was practice babe?" I asked him, kissing him on the lips.

"It was straight. How were the *Sunbeams*?" He laughed.

"It was coo. I met this girl Karen, she was sweet."

"Brown skin chick?" He asked, frowning his face up.

"Yeah. Why you looking like that?"

"Nothing," he answered, heading up the stairs.

Dismissing it, I let it go. "You know anybody drive a black Jetta?" I asked, walking up the stairs.

"What that bitch tell you Germany?" He asked, coming from around the corner looking irritated as hell.

"What bitch Herahm."

"Karen!" He replied.

"Nothing Herahm, I swear. I only asked because I saw one following behind me today."

He took a long stare into my eyes. "You okay?" I asked, putting my hand on my hip.

"I'm straight, go get ready for the event."

Turning on his heels, he headed towards the bedroom leaving me to ponder over what just occurred.

Something aint right, but I'm fasho gone find out.

Dressing in silence, we were both ready to leave within the hour. A cream turtle neck crop top sweater on my back. Leather garter leggings were on my ass, paired with black Christian Louboutin Maillot booties. My hair was flat ironed and parted down the middle.

Rolling up to the club thirty minutes later, we were photographed as soon as we stepped out the car.

Non stop flashing of the cameras as we walked straight through the double doors.

Good Pussy by Joe Moses was blaring out the speakers. The vibe was super chill as we made our way to the VIP section.

"Heeeey Herahm!" I heard some groupies say to him.

Nodding his head to em, he grabbed my hand and led me in front of him. Winking my eye to the bitches, I took a seat on the couch.

"Germany! Hey!" I heard a voice yelling over the music. Karen was walking towards us in a bright red bandage dress.

"Hi Karen!" I greeted, standing to reciprocate her cheek kiss.

"Twice in one day." She laughed.

"Have a seat," I said, waving her down to have a seat.

"Babe I'll be right back." Herahm said, walking away as soon as Karen had a seat.

Rolling my eyes, I sipped on the champagne at the waiter brought.

"How long you been here?" She asked, taking the seat Herahm vacated.

"Less than thirty minutes. Your boyfriend here?"

"Yeah, he's over there with your man."

"Roman Lakes?"

"Yup." She replied, pointing to the mixed dude with the braids standing next to Herahm.

"Oh ok cool."

"Tonight is our two year anniversary," she grinned from ear to ear.

"Aww congrats," I replied, genuinely happy for her love.

"How long you and Herahm been together?"

"About six seven months." I replied.

"That's cute. Where do you see your relationship going?" She quizzed. "You know how these celebrity relationships go. Be having babies on the way but out in clubs and in the media with other bitches and shit."

The way she said it caught me off guard.

"Good thing I don't have those problems," I replied in a joking way, trying to ease the uneasiness that entered the room.

Karen got up shortly after and hit the dance floor. She was on the dance floor, putting on a show. She had all eyes on her as she moved her body as if she got paid to do it. Popping her ass, I couldn't help but to laugh as all eyes were on her.

Deciding to join in on the attention, I grabbed Herahm, and headed to the dance floor. I starting grinding on him and everybody started going crazy.

They turned the spotlight on us and numerous cameras were being pointed at us as we enjoyed each other.

Drop That Kitty by Ty Dolla Sign was playing. I had my ass dropping like hydraulics one cheek at a time.

Herahm was keeping up as I twerked my ass off. My hair was swinging from side to side and I couldn't do anything but enjoy the movement. I was finally living!

Chapter Nineteen

Retail therapy was my only desire for the day. *Timea's Boutique* was my first destination, and when I came across a Faux Leather white trimmed dress that I had to have. It was long sleeve with allover ruching that I loved. I went through racks and racks of clothes finding a bunch of things that I absolutely adored. When I came across the leather mid-calf pencil skirt, I knew that would come in handy. The sleek stretch crepe jersey fabric was beautiful.

Finding a mock turtleneck two tone black and white dress, with long sleeve, I knew if I didn't hurry up and leave, I'd be shopping all day.

Grabbing a pair of black Giuseppe Zanotti crystal-coated suede platform sandals, I had to pull myself from the store.

After paying for my purchases, I was in my own world trying to figure out where I'd get something to eat from when I accidentally bumped into someone. "Excuse me!" I said, looking up.

"Germany?" How are you?"

"Hi Karen, I'm good, and you?"

"I'm good. What you doing?"

"Just finished shopping, about to stop somewhere to eat. Care to join?"

"Sure."

We made our way to the Italian restaurant across the street and had a seat.

"I'm loving the jumpsuit you're wearing," I complimented, giving her the once over. Bright red color that she paired gold accessories with. Hair in a tight bun, with gold studs in her ear.

"Can I start you ladies off with a drink?" the waiter asked, pen and pad ready.

"I'll have a bay breeze," I ordered.

"And for you m'am?"

"I'll take a strawberry daiquiri."

"Do you still need a minute to order your food or you ready?" He asked, looking between the both of us.

"I know what I want," I laughed, looking over at Karen who was still glazing over the menu. "I'll have the chicken parmesan with sundried tomatoes and light alfredo sauce. Fresh Caesar salad with bacon bits please." I handed him the menu and grabbed for my mirror in my purse to check my lipstick.

"I'll have the spaghetti with olives, tomatoes and basil. Fresh black pepper and garlic toast please."

Handing him the menu, she then looked towards me.

"How has your day been going?" she started.

"I'm sorry I responded," as my phone rang. Looking down, I noticed it was my Mother.

"Yes Mom," I answered.

"I love you Germany."

"I love you too Mom."

"I just got off the phone with Herahm and he is a lovely boy."

"You just got off the phone with Herahm? About what?"

"He's having a birthday party and he wanted to invite me."

"Well that was nice."

"Germany, you and I need to talk about what happened."

"Mom not now, I'm at lunch so we can discuss this later."

Click.

"Everything okay?" She asked, sipping on her drink. The waiter came out with our food and it was a needed distraction.

"Any sauces needed?" He asked.

"No thank you," I responded.

He walked away, and I picked over my food.

"You okay?" Karen repeated, looking concerned.

"I'm fine. Herahm invited my Mom to his birthday party next Saturday and I had no idea."

"That's sweet though. He clearly is invested if he's inviting Mom's out." She responded.

"That's true. My Mother and I just aren't in the best of spaces right now so it's a little rocky."

"I understand, just focus on the positive part which is your relationship."

"I appreciate that."

"Not to pry, but you haven't had any scandals in the media have you?"

"Hell nah, and I don't plan too."

"How'd you two meet?"

"We met at a basketball game two years ago. How'd you and your man meet?"

"We went to school together. Herahm too. We were all a close group of friends," she revealed.

"Oh wow, I had no idea." The wheels got to turning in my head.

"Yeah, so you said two years ago? But I thought you said y'all only been dating for about seven months."

"That's correct. We met briefly, nothing happened. Ran into each other again years later, and here we are."

I can see the wheels turning around in her head and I was getting uneasy.

"Did you fuck my nigga?" I asked her bluntly, getting amped up.

"Eww no," she said, rolling her eyes.

"You sure, because you questioning me like it's something you hinting around too."

"No Germany, there's no issue. Just putting a timeline together," she winked, getting from the table.

"Look bitch, I don't know what the fuck is going on, but if it's something you gotta say, let it out."

"Oh it'll be let out. Soon!"

Chapter Twenty

"We are here," the driver said as he pulled up to the *Staples Center* in Los Angeles. Herahm had pulled out all the stops for the night, even having an authentic red carpet being laid out for myself and him to walk on when arriving. Paparazzi were on standby, awaiting our arrival for the evening, which made the night even more special.

Tonight was one for the tabloids for sure.

"Herahm really went all out for this huh?" My Mom said, as we sat idly in the car.

"Yes he did," I said as the butterflies shifted in my stomach.

"Germany, you and still never got to discuss what happened the day of breakfast-"

"Stop ma," I cut her off. "It's not up for discussion. Tonight is Herahm's birthday and I don't want to spoil it."

Nodding her head, she exited the car when the driver opened the door and I followed suit.

While taking numerous pictures, Herahm's white Phantom pulled up. My King emerged and took my breath away.

The bubble gum pink one shoulder Galliono gown I wore was stunning. Accentuated with the diamond necklace around my neck, I was giving old Hollywood Glamour.

The Jimmy Choo pumps I had on made my already long legs even more enticing. Herahm joined me in front of the cameras and the love I saw in his eyes were enough to let me know he loved me unconditionally.

"Happy birthday baby!" I yelled into the camera, spraying him with silly string.

It seemed as if a thousand light bulbs went off as the paparazzi had a field day capturing photos of us gazing into each other's eyes. He grabbed for my arm and we took loads of pictures together, posing like jailbirds.

Just enjoying the moment.

The décor of the room was amazing with the red, pink, and white roses that decorated the room. Huge ice sculptures were put up throughout the room. A white piano suspended in midair with a beautiful lady playing it was the icing on the cake. The party looked like something Diddy who was in attendance would throw.

Herahm led me further into the room and when I noticed one familiar face in particular, I teared up.

"Miss Janet!" I yelled, as she embraced me. "How are you?"

"I'm fine. How are you beautiful?"

"I'm good. What are you doing here?"

"Your mother invited me," she responded, nodding her head in my Mother's direction.

"I just want to tell you thank you." I said, hugging her again.

"You are so welcome baby." She said, hugging me back.

There were at least three hundred people in the building. Half friends, associates, celebrities and family. More than half being Herahm's. It was a white affair. Everyone in attendance was given orders to wear only white. Herahm made sure he and I were the focus of tonight.

Herahm in a black Tom Ford suit with pink accents that was tailored to perfection. I mingled and spoke to old friends and family members.

I was glad Herahm made the decision to have everyone wear white. We were obviously the stand outs of the party, and it was easy to spot him out the crowd when I needed him. I garnered so many compliments as I floated around the room as if I was on a cloud.

When Herahm made his way back to me, I asked him to the dance floor and we began to dance like true lovers.

"Aww they are so cute," I heard Herahm's sister whisper.

We continued to dance until Herahm's mother cleared her throat and spoke into the mic.

The lights dimmed and the spotlight fell upon us as he led me to the podium in front of everyone.

"Herahm Santana, you are the epitome of what I desired you to be as a son. The unconditional love, drive and happiness you bring to my life makes me the happiest mother in the world. Everyday for the past 25 years, you have made me the proudest mother ever. Your drive to accomplish your dreams, not only for yourself but for your family." Her voice started to crack a little.

"I know all of our days haven't been picture perfect. The days when Mama couldn't afford to keep the lights on. It all shaped you into the amazing man you are." "Happy Birthday son." She concluded.

Leading me towards his mother, he took a knee at the seat she was sitting in to give his mother a hug.

Grabbing the mic from her, he said "I love you mama. You are the greatest gift God has ever bestowed upon me. Everyone was clapping as they embraced."

Turning towards me, I looked into my eyes. "Would you give me the greatest pleasure of all by allowing me to be your husband?" He asked, pulling out a ring box from the inside of his blazer.

Tears fell out of my eyes as I answered "Yes," to my proposal. There wasn't a dry eye in sight as we kissed and were officially engaged.

"You had this all planned out huh?" I asked as we made our way out of the *Staples Center*.

"I did. You are one step closer to becoming Mrs. Herahm Santana."

The party filed out with us as we headed toward the car.

"This is pure bliss." I said kissing him on the lips. Herahm hopped in the drivers side and I got in the passenger. Just as he was getting ready to pull off, a black Jetta swerved in front of us.

A bitch hopped out the car and I did the exact same.

"Aint yall so fucking cute!"

Standing in the middle of the street was a lightskin bitch who looked like she was ready to pop. Her stomach hung over her jeans as she waddled her pregnant ass towards us.

The cameras were catching everything.

"You told ya bitch you got twins on the way Herahm?" the bitch said once he hopped out the car.

"Bitch what?"

It was the bitch from the Nail Shop. Then it all started coming to me.

"Bitch that was you following me?! I'm finna fuck this bitch up!"

I was boiling over with anger.

"Samantha get the fuck out of here. Them aint my babies."

"You was fucking the bitch?" I asked, turning my attention to him. My heart was beating a mile a minute and I knew I had to be dreaming. This was a nightmare.

"He the sure the fuck was." Karen emerged from out of the Jetta and I lost it. Before she knew what hit her, I rushed her and punched her in the nose. Blood gushed from her nose, as I followed that with two jabs to her eye. She started swinging like a mad woman as I side stepped a wild left she threw at me. Grabbing a handful of her hair, I wrapped it around my fist and yanked that ass down. Two uppercuts were what she felt as I let that ass fall to the ground.

Herahm came running to the other side of the car to grabbed me off the bitch.

Boop! I stole on his ass too. Running to the driver's side, I hopped in the car as the cameras went crazy. I peeled out the parking lot leaving behind my life in the rearview.

Seduced.

"Breaking, basketball star Herahm Santana and longtime girlfriend Germany-Skyy break up right after getting engaged.

Video has surfaced of Germany getting into a bad altercation with point guard Roman Lakes girlfriend Karen Jones after finding out Santana fathered another child with ex Samantha Hernandez."

I'm on every channel, I rolled my eyes as I turned from the television off. My eyes were puffy from crying so much and I didn't know what to do.

My phone had been ringing non stop. Herahm had been blowing me and that was the last person I wanted to hear from.

Leaving me about a dozen messages, I hadn't returned one call.

Hiding out at Four Seasons for the pass week, I was avoiding any and everyone.

The text tone of my phone going off grabbed my attention.

Germany I'm sure there are no words I can share with you that will take away the pain you feel. I am sorry and I know that doesn't mean anything, but please give me a chance to make this right. I love you and I want to be with you. I'll do anything you want. I can get you in any movie, start you a clothing line, help you model. Anything. Just give me a chance to make this right. It read.

Okay mothafucka, you want to embarrass me, I'll do the same. I thought, plotting on his ass.

Meet me at the park we met at in Oakland tonight. Midnight, I texted him.

Dialing Brooklyn, I paced the hotel room until she answered the phone.

"What you doing fatty?"

"Laying down, this niece of yours is doing too much." She laughed into the phone. "How you doing Germany? Maurice been talking to Herahm and that boy going crazy."

"I'm fine. Do you still have that video camera you used to have."

"Yeah, I just pulled it out for Maurice because he wanna film the baby birth."

"Can I borrow it?"

"For?"

"I just need it sis, can I borrow it?"

"Yeah, when you coming to get it?"

"How much battery life does it hold?"

"Four hours on a full charge." She responded. Looking at the clock, I had perfect timing.

"I'm on my way to get it now."

"K."

I had a little under two hours to execute my plan.

I exited the hotel, trying to not draw any attention to myself. Hopping in the Audi, I raced to Brooklyn's house.

Hugging me when she opened the front door, she just stared in my eyes.

"You okay Germany?"

Nodding my head, I rubbed her stomach.

"I love you Brooklyn, I just want you to know that."

"I love you too and you'll get through this. Just stay away from Herahm." She warned.

Not answering her, I reached for the camera.

"Did you hear me Germany?"

"Yes Brooklyn."

"I'm serious. Maurice said he been talking crazy on some suicidal type of shit. You just need to stay away and focus on rebuilding yourself up."

"I hear you sis. I gotta get outta here." I wasn't in the mood to hear that shit. I had my mind on only one thing and that was revenge.

I pulled up to the park and put my plan in motion. Parking my car, I got out and set the camera up to face the lot where Herahm and I will be. Hiding in the shadows of the bushes, but still being able to capture everything, it was on.

"Nigga want to play with me, I got you." I thought.

Herahm pulled up as soon as the clock struck midnight. My heart skipped a beat as I watched him whip his Ferrari into the deserted lot. Exiting my car, I glanced over at the camera before I strutted to his car and entered the passenger side.

Paranoid by Ty Dolla Sign played softly in the background. The song was definitely befitting for the occasion, since the last time I was in the presence of him, we were not on the best of terms. My instincts were at an all-time high and something about this situation didn't feel right to me. My instincts had never steered me wrong before, and I just couldn't shake the nerves.

"Germany!" He said, pulling me out of my thoughts.

"Wassup Herahm? What is it exactly that you need to say to me?" I asked.

"I have you out here to see if we could possibly fix what was broken in our relationship."

"Herahm, you have to be fucking kidding me! You cheated on me and got a bitch pregnant! You really think I want yo dirty dick ass after some shit like that? Get the fuck outta here." I rolled my eyes at his black ass and turned my head.

"Look Germany, I don't know how many times I have to apologize to make this right, but I can't or won't live without you."

There was a underlying message in what he just said, and I felt it.

"You don't have a choice, because I'm all the way done. You don't even realize how much I loved you. Would have done anything for you! I worshipped the ground you walked on. When you were happy, I was happy. When you were hurting, so was I. Your smile made me melt. The way you held me made me weak. The way you touched me drove me crazy."

Tears began falling at this point, but I finally had the chance to tell him how much he hurt me and I couldn't stop.

"I don't want you anymore Herahm," I finished, wiping the tears from my eyes. "I asked you that day we were in the bed when I woke up in the middle of the night to not hurt me. And this is the shit you do!"

"Germany, I'm sorry, please believe me. Do you remember the first time we met? It was two years ago in the same park we're in right now. Why you think I brought you here? I want to fix this."

"NO! What the fuck did I just tell you. There is nothing to fucking fix! It's over, so shut the fuck up talking to me! I gotta get the fuck outta here," I yelled. All the hatred I had for him began bubbling to the surface, and I needed this nigga out of my presence.

"Germany-Skyy Santana!" He started, adding fuel to the fire.

"If you don't shut the fuck up, I'm getting the fuck out."

"You better stop cutting me off while I'm fucking talking!" He warned, before continuing, "like I was about to say, I won't live without you Germany. You belong to me!" A crazy look glazed over his eyes and it was unsettling.

"Fuck it, I'm gone." I spat in his face and flung my door open.

"Germany!" he yelled, hopping out of the car behind me.

I continued walking and never turned around to see whether he was following behind me or not. The sounds of my Jimmy Choos click clacking on the pavement beneath me sounded off in the deserted lot. By time I finally turned around, it was too late.

BAM! He hit me on the side of my head with the butt of his gun. I went crashing straight to the ground.

Oh my god, he's going to kill me, was the first thought that crossed my mind.

"Bitch I tried to keep it simple with yo mu'fucking ass, but you just don't know how to act. I told you I wouldn't live without you and I meant that shit." He stood above me with his silver plated pistol pointing directly at my mouth.

"I'mma pop you right in yo fucking grill since yo mouth so fucking greasy."

Why didn't I listen to Brooklyn? I thought, tears streaming down my face.

Before I could even beg for my life the next thing I heard was the blast of a gun. My eyes were closed and I just knew it was all over.

But when I opened my eyes and the zeroed in on the face standing above me with the smoking gun, I knew it all had finally caught to me.

"Well hello Germany, longtime no see."

"Sincere!" I whispered right before his gun let off.

Seducing
The Hustle

Bronchey Ju'Tone Sair

Chapter One

2008

Walking in the house I found my mother sprawled out on the kitchen floor. There was a bottle of Taaka Vodka in one hand while she puffed on an almost finished cigarette in the other. Looking around the dirty cramped apartment we stayed in, located in the Hunters Point projects in San Francisco, I shook my head in disgust as I headed for my room.

Bypassing my mom on the floor, I took a second look at her. Her once jet black curls that spiraled to the middle of her back were now thin and straggly looking. Her once glowing high yellow complexion had now taken on an ashy look. The beautiful curves that she once possessed were now a pile of chicken bones. The sparkle behind her hazel eyes had now dimmed. The once envied Queen to the *King of the streets* had fallen victim to the environment that surrounded her life.

Shaking my head, I stepped over her and went into my room. Picking up boxers, jeans, and t-shirts, I began to clean the dungeon I called my room. Picking up sneakers to put back in their boxes, I could hear my mom calling me from the living room.

Dropping my shoes on the floor, I opened the door to my room to see what she wanted.

"What?" I asked, standing in the doorway that led to the living room.

"You've grown to become a smart, intelligent, and handsome young man HaKoda. If your Daddy was still here, booooy it'd be something crazy," She said, looking at me as if she hadn't seen me in years.

"Thanks ma." I responded, turning back around to go into my room.

"I'M NOT FINISHED TALKING TO YOU HaKoda! AND SINCE YOU WANNA BE DISRESPECTFUL BY WALKING AWAY WHILE I'M STILL TALKING, I GOT SOME WORDS FOR YO MU'FUCKIN ASS. You need to start bringing some more money up in here. I'm getting up there in age and I can't continue doing the shit I been doing to make money so you need to get out there and do something."

"Look ma. I'm not trying to hear 'bout none of dat shit you be doing. I bring what I can in here from working at the barbershop and I'm doing that underhanded. I'm seventeen and shit but damn. I'm making about six hundred a month and I'm giving you half. What else do you need from me?"

"More NIGGA!"

"If Dad was still here you wouldn't be on me like this. But since you checked outta life after he passed, you just don't give a fuck? GET YO JUNKIE ASS OFF THAT SHIT YOU SMOKING, AND THERE'D BE MORE MONEY IN THIS MOTHA'FUCKA. Uncle Ahmed pays the rent out this raggedy mu'fucka, and you get a SSI check every month."

After having to pretty much raise myself after my Dad died, I'd lost the majority of respect I once held for my mother. She let the drugs turn her out, and it cost her, our relationship. I love my Mother more than life, but I hold so much resentment towards her.

"Check this out nigga. Regardless of how you feel, this raggedy mu'fucka is mine! And you're going to watch your mouth talking to me like that. I am still your mama!!"

"Act like it then."

"I'm going to say this and then I'm done." She said, getting in my face. My 6'1" frame towered over her 5'6" self as she talked to my chest. "I'm giving you until the first of next month to start bringing in some more money or you can get the fuck out of my spot."

"So, what, you going to put me out?"

"I sure the fuck am! I want a thousand dollars by the first."

"That's two weeks."

"Make it happen. You better have Ahmed snake ass give it too you!" With that, her skeletal body made her way to the filth infested place she called a room.

She scratched at her arms hard, drawing blood as she slammed the door shut to her room. I knew that if I didn't get my cake up, I'd be homeless. It wasn't even about bringing money in here to help out. She wanted more money so I could help feed her habit. Although I had tried to refrain from entering the street life, the only way I'd be able to bring in a *G* a month, I'd have to enter the game.

"What's good nephew?" my Uncle Ahmed asked, as we dapped hands.

"Nothing man."

"C'mon nephew. You know I know you better than that. What's going on?" he asked, taking a seat at his kitchen table. Uncle Ahmed was the definition of an old school player. Hustling major weight back in the day for my Dad, the only thing is, he didn't do what my dad asked him to do if something happened to him. He wasn't taking care of us. He took the money he used from his illegal activities and opened up a few businesses around the area. Sporting a short fade, with diamonds in both ears. *He's clearly living with no worries, but we're out here struggling. Cold World.*

After it went down that day at the court house, Unc Ahmed was now a retired veteran who could teach me the *ins-and-outs* of the game.

"I'm going to be all the way straight with you. I need a plug man. Shit has been getting hectic and I need some real type of paper coming through. You feel me?" I said, getting to the point of my visit.

"HaKoda. The reason I haven't taken you under my wing the way I want to is because I know you to be a lot smarter than the average nigga your age. You fought the allure of the game after everything went down at the trial. You're too good for the streets. It's in your blood, but it's not for you. What got you chasing the life all of a sudden?" He quizzed, giving me his undivided attention.

"It's a long story that I don't feel like getting into right now. But is there anybody you know that's looking for a worker, because this is important."

"What if I gave you a raise?"

"Check this out Unc, unless you trying to throw a couple bands to ya' boi every month, there isn't much you can do but to help me get in touch with somebody that can put me on." I responded as respectfully as I could. Resorting to this life was not my ideal lifestyle choice, but my Moms left no alternative.

"I'll see what I can do." He responded, just as a black BMW M3 pulled up in front of the house. My mouth was drooling as I lusted over the beautiful automobile.

"Whose whip is that?" I asked, as I waited to see who was going to get out the car.

"My young nigga La'Ron. Actually, this nigga might be the man to help you with your situation."

"With a whip like that, shit I hope so," I commented as I watched Ahmed head out front to meet La'Ron.

Once I get on my feet, imma have my shit just like that, I thought.

Uncle Ahmed hit me with some news that La'Ron was willing to work me ONLY off the strength him.

Jumping head first into the game without the proper knowledge or grooming, I was like a mouse in a cage full of snakes. Reputation to be known, La'Ron was a crazy nigga that didn't play when it came to business and money. I had to be on my P's and Q's when I started working for him.

Chapter Two

Pittsburg High, *the home of the Pirates*. My stomping grounds.

Making a transaction right before my eyes, I watched from afar as Dammar made his sell on the corner of School Street. Dapping hands, they exchanged the drugs and money. They did it so smoothly, that to the untrained eye, they looked as if they were just showing each other love.

"What's poppin' wit my nigga HaKoda?" He asked walked towards me?

Standing at the Creative Arts building stairs, we dapped hands.

Dressed in black True Religion jeans, and a black short sleeve button up, he was fresh. The Air Jordan 12 playoffs were on his feet. Freshly faded haircut accompanied with enough waves to make a sea sick.

"Same shit different day. I can't call it." I responded, as watching his customer head down the steps to join the crowd of students forming to enter the school. I didn't have the most money in the world, but one thing I never slacked on was my apparel. A pair of black Levi jeans on my ass, a short sleeve Burberry button up courtesy of the local booster, and black suede Timberlands on my feet.

My shoulder length dreads were braided into a Mohawk going to the back of my head. Caramel complexion with a single dimple in my left cheek. Hazel eyed nigga with light freckles, standing at 6'1" at the age of 17.

"So word around town is, niggas finna start fuckin wit La'Ron. What's good?"

"Who you hear dat shit from?"

Dammar and I had grown up together, and were pretty cool although he slung that shit and I didn't. Him being a dope boy and me being a straight-laced student, we had different views of life. He knew of my situation at home, and had even looked out for me a few times.

"C'mon bruh, you know mu'fuckas talk."

"Nah bro, it ain't nothing too serious. Just some slight shit."

"Yeah whatever nigga, just be safe. If you need anything, you already know."

"I'm already knowing" I replied, dapping hands with him as the school bell signaled our moment of departure.

When that *3:03pm* bell rang, I couldn't sprint out of Miss Jenkins' English class fast enough! Time wasn't necessarily on my side, and the faster I linked up with La'Ron, the better. Walking to

Angelo's off Harbor St, I noticed La'Ron's Benz driving towards the store.

All the hoes from the school went flockin to his car.

Rolling the window down, he looked straight at me.

"Hop in bro."

Without hesitation, I hopped into the front seat. All eyes were on us as he turned his music up. *"Fuck U Gon Do 'Bout It"* by Plies was blaring out the speakers.

"I'll check you later," I hollered to Dammar as we sped off. My body melted into the soft peanut leather seats as we hit the streets.

"So I hear you looking to be put on." La'Ron said, keeping his eyes on the road. Looking from the Rolex on his wrist, and the diamonds glistening in his ears, I was certain he could teach me a thing or two.

"I am. I need this shit bad too."

"Yo Uncle told me a lil about ya situation at the house with your moms. I had that exact situation, so I see where the motivation to **get it** is coming from." His eyes left the road as he looked me over.

"Yeah its crazy man, but I gotta get it the best way I can." I said, looking him dead in the eye.

"I hear you bruh, I definitely do. But ya Unc also let it be known, you're very intelligent and you're better than these streets. So what I'm going to do is be my cash handler. What that'll entail is you going to pick up my dough from around the city and bring it to me. Nothing too crazy."

"Good looking." I responded.

The conversation slowly died after that. Plaguing me, I asked, "Hold old is you man?" Judging by his looks, dude could only be a few years older than me. He had a short tapered fro, chocolate complexion, and a goatee.

"Nineteen."

"Oh okay cool."

"I'm going to have you start working tomorrow."

"Perfect." And just like that, a hustler was born.

Gangsta' Bitch

The Mei'Yari Lewis story

Bronchey Ju'Tone Sair

Chapter One
Hood Shit

Richmond, CA

I could hear screaming coming from the inside of my apartment as I walked up the concrete stairs. I shook my head at the ghetto-ness of the situation as I put my keys in the door to let myself inside. My mother was lying on the kitchen floor bleeding from the huge gash on her forehead. My dad was standing on top of her with a skillet in his hands.

"Bitch didn't I tell you to have my fucking dinner ready by time I got home? It's four fucking o'clock and you just now getting ready to start cooking this shit!"

"Mike you told me you'd be home by six. I thought I had enough time to have your dinner ready by time you got here. I promise it won't happen again!" My Mom pleaded.

"I'm sick of these fucking excuses Diane. You always got some excuse as to why the shit not done. I'm tired of this shit!" My dad had a deranged look in his face and I was frozen in place as he started kicking my mom in the abdomen. My Mom was seven months pregnant with my baby brother and to see him treat her that way had me ready to go postal.

"Daddy stop! I'm so fucking sick and tired of you coming in here putting your hands on us. How about you just take yo drunk ass somewhere else and leave us the fuck alone!" My dad was an alcoholic upset with his own life. One dead end job after another was the root of all his problems. I was up to my last straw with this bullshit. I had seen my Mom receive more ass whoopings and black eyes then any indication of love that I could remember. There weren't any peaceful moments in the Lewis household and if shit didn't change quick, I knew somebody was going to end up dead.

"Bitch what the fuck yo lil fast ass say to me?" My Mom's eyes looked from him to me as he turned his rage to me.

"No Mei'Yari, it's okay. Just go in your room and everything will be ok."

"No Mom, fuck that! This sorry excuse for a man needs to get the fuck up outta here. I'm tired of this shit!"

"Oh you think you grown now huh? Done started having sex and you think you can say anything you want to me huh?" He was looking at me with a perverted look in his eye and it was very unsettling. "Well imma show you just how grown you really are!" This nigga started pulling at my shirt like he was about to rape me.

Fear paralyzed me as he started pulling me to the ground. It took about a second after he pulled my blouse off of me leaving me standing in the living room in my black lace bra for me to start fighting him back. When I heard my thirteen year old brother Sair come from out of his room crying for my dad to stop, that was what made me start fighting harder. I couldn't watch let my brother watch me get raped. I was fighting to the death. He started fumbling with his jeans as I clawed at his face. "Get the fuck up off of me!" I yelled.

"Nah bitch, you want to be grown? Imma show you grown!"

As I continued to wrestle with him, I saw my Mom coming from behind him holding a butchers knife. "Fuck you Mike! I fucking hate you!" She yelled right before she stabbed him in his back. He rolled off of me just as my Mom brought the knife back down in his stomach. She had snapped and as she continued to stab him, I crawled into a corner in the living-room as the severity of what I just happened and what could've happened became a reality. I watched my dad who had just attempted to rape me, take his last breath as the blade of the knife exited and reentered his body.

I was in a daze when I heard bamming on the front door. I sat completely still as my Mother continued to stab my father's lifeless body. When the front door came crashing in and two uniformed police officers rushed in with their guns drawn, I just sat there with tears in my eyes.

"M'am please drop your weapon. Everything is ok, just please put the knife down."

My Mom drop to her knees clutching her stomach as blood started oozing down her legs. Sair rushed to her side with tears free falling from his eyes. She was yelling out in pain as the white officer put her in handcuffs.

"Call an ambulance!" I yelled as the officers tried to pull her to her feet. The blood was now running like a faucet down her leg and I was scared that she was about to miscarry the baby. The black officer asked for a bus in his walkie talkie as they attempted to calm my Mom down.

"The ambulance is three minutes away, everything will be ok. Will you be able to tell me what has gone on here m'am?" Asked the white police officer. He looked like he was more interested in the crime scene then my Mom's health.

"I... I don't give a fuck about what has gone on here!" My Mom said, huffing and puffing. "Just get me into the fucking ambulance and get these fucking cuffs off of me!"

I heard the sirens of the fire truck and ambulance getting closer to our apartment as I said a quick prayer to God to get my Mom and brother through this. Once the ambulance came inside our apartment and put my Mom up on the gurney, something in my heart told me everything would be okay.

In the back of the ambulance, we flew through the streets at top speed to get my Mom to the hospital. I held on to my Moms hand tightly as the EMT attempted to stop the bleeding. My Mom's face was contorted up in pain as she felt the baby losing consciousness in her womb. "Please hurry up, I can feel the baby suffocating! Please help me deliver this baby!" She cried.

As many times as I had seen my Mother cry, none was ever as painful as this. The pain was resonating from her heart and as they attempted to deliver my brother, I closed my eyes and continued to pray that everything would be fine.

They made me wait in the visiting room in the hospital as my Mom gave birth prematurely. She wasn't due for another two months and the chances of my brother surviving were very slim. I was pacing back and forth the entire time hoping and praying everything would be fine. Hours passed before someone came out of my Mother's delivery room to let me and Sair know that she had delivered a five pound and seven ounce baby.

Tears of joy rolled down my rosy cheeks as I was led into her delivery room. I held on to Sair's hand tightly as we took in our Mother's appearance. She was sleeping with bandages wrapped around her bruised ribs and head. She looked as if she was finally at peace, and when I walked over to my baby brother inside the hospital issued bassinet the water works started. He was so beautiful and all I could do was thank God that both he and my Mom had pulled through. Our dad was out of the picture and I knew we could finally be out peace.

At least that was what I was thinking when the same white officer who had come to our house came strolling into the room. "Diane Lewis, you are under arrest for the murder of Michael Lee Lewis. You have the right to remain silent. Anything you say can and will be used against you in the court of law. You have the right to an attorney. If you cannot afford an attorney, one will be appointed to you."

My Mom wasn't coherent as he read her her rights and my anger hit an all time high as I got in the officer's face.

"What the fuck do you mean she's under arrest? She killed my father in self-defense and you know it!"

"Get your little black ass out of my face before I lock your ass up too. Your mother is under arrest so sit down and shut the fuck up!"

"Fuck you!" I spat in his face and turned on my heels as he put my mother in handcuffs. *He gone get his,* I thought as I left the hospital without a backwards glance. Leaving Sair alone to fend for himself was the hardest thing I ever had to do, but I knew we'd be reunited. It was fate.

Chapter Two
The Up and Up

These niggas thought just because I was a female they could get over on me! What they didn't know was I am the baddest bitch to ever do it and for their treachery they'd have to be dealt with, I thought, as I sat in the rented Lincoln town car with my twin desert eagles seated in the passengers seat. I was watching the house where the niggas who robbed me stayed, and my trigger finger was itching. *I can't wait to get my shit back,* I thought.

I sat back and thought about what had got me in the position I was in and shook my head. After leaving the hospital I hit the ground hard on a paper chase. I wasn't sure how I would survive with my Mom possibly going to prison so I did what I felt was natural to me. I started hustling. I knew my boyfriend Ju'Tone was heavy in the dope game so I did what I needed to do. I sucked and fuck that nigga so good he was glad to hand over some work for me. By time my mom's trial came up, I had already started my come up. I was living a little better, and I had a few stacks saved and I was counting on my mom getting out so I could take care of her.

I felt as if I was having an out of body experience when they handed my Mom eight years for voluntary manslaughter. Although the bruises she and I had endured and showed, the judge felt as if killing my father wasn't enough of a punishment. He wanted her to suffer for a little while. My Mother mouthed to me that she'd be okay as she was led out of the courtroom. I knew she would be, but who I was really worried about was my baby brother. He would be lost in the system because I wasn't old enough to take care of him. I left the courthouse a brand new woman. Cash and vengeance was the only things I thought about from that day on.

The day the niggas robbed me for my shit was the day I became a full-fledged hustler, and I guess I was going to have to show these niggas I went just as hard as any nigga. *Maybe harder!*

I had been watching that house for about four hours waiting to make my move. Word around the hood was that the niggas who robbed me for my shit lived inside the house. Ju'Tone wanted to send some of his goons to retrieve his shit but I assured him everything would be taken care of. Grabbing both of my guns I clicked the safety off them both. Twisting the silencers on them, I was ready to get it popping. Just as I was about to hop out of the car my phone began buzzing. *Fuck!* I thought as I answered.

"Hello?" I answered with major attitude.

"Bitch, what the fuck is you doing?" My girl Lola replied, sounding extra ghetto.

"I'm kind of busy so I'll call you back." I told her trying to rush her off the phone.

"Girl I know you not still tripping over that shit that happened with them niggas. You'll just have to take it as a loss and start over." She began saying.

"Sorry but I didn't ask for your opinion."
Click.

Fuck she mean, 'take it as a loss?' That was eight ounces of coke and ten thousand dollars in cash. Bitch must be out of her mind.

I was overly pissed now and was ready to get this shit over with. Double checking my guns, I hopped out of the car. My 5'7" frame was covered in all black with my honey blonde hair pulled into a bun underneath a ball cap. If anyone was to see me which I doubt being that it was pitch black outside courtesy of the broken street lights and the time, I'd probably look like a teen boy.

Getting to the house, I went around the back to check the windows. Looking inside I could see one of the men who robbed me sitting in the bedroom. He was dumping money and drugs onto the bed as I continued watching him. Just the sight of him made me want to pop him where he stood.

"Man that nigga Ritchie was really holding!" he exclaimed, looking over his shoulder to talk to his partner.

"Damn they got my nigga Ritchie too!" I whispered. *Theses niggas just robbing everybody,* I thought.

Leaving the money on the bed he took the pistol from his waistband and also dropped that onto the bed. Going into the living room, he and the other guy were out of sight. With both guns in my hands I walked to the front of the house. Walking straight up to the front door I let off two rounds into the door and kicked it in.

Bam! The door swung open. Both men were unprepared as I hit the man with braids I seen inside the bedroom with two shots to the chest and two to the dome.

The other man dressed in a wife beater, blue jeans and timberlands was able to dive behind the couch. He let off two shots landing two inches above my head in the wall behind me.

"Stupid mu'fucka!" I yelled as I hit him once between the eyes. His body made a loud thud as I raced into the bedroom. I hurried into the room to get my shit. I grabbed the duffle bag and started putting all the money and drugs dude had put onto the bed back inside the bag. I was dashing out of the room when I dropped a stack of money on the floor. *Jackpot.*

There were more duffle bags underneath the bed. When I opened one, there was nothing but drugs inside. Opening another, there was money inside. Originally I had only come to get what I was owed, but seeing the opportunity I was being handed, I decided to take it all. There were three bags underneath the bed, not counting the bag I already had in my hands.

After three trips to and from the car, I sped away with more money and drugs then I'd ever touched. Once I got home, I sat down and counted all the money I had stolen from their house. After an hour of counting and recounting, I had come up with a *$250,000* in cash without adding the four kilos of coke in the other bags. I stayed up the remainder of the night formulating a plan on how I was going to go from nothing to something overnight. I was on my way to the top!

Gangsta
The Sair Lewis story

Bronchey Sair

He's Coming!

Made in the USA
Columbia, SC
24 September 2018